# O'Dwyer & Grady

## STARRING IN

# TOUGH ACT TO FOLLOW

# O'Dwyer & Grady

## STARRING IN

# TOUGH ACT TO FOLLOW

## By Eileen Heyes

*Eileen Heyes*

**Aladdin Paperbacks**
New York London Toronto Sydney Singapore

This book is a work of fiction. Any references to historical events, real people, or real locales are used fictitiously. Other names, characters, places, and incidents are the product of the author's imagination, and any resemblance to actual events or locales or persons, living or dead, is entirely coincidental.

First Aladdin Paperbacks edition June 2003
Copyright © 2003 by Eileen Heyes

ALADDIN PAPERBACKS
An imprint of Simon & Schuster
Children's Publishing Division
1230 Avenue of the Americas
New York, NY 10020

Designed by Lisa Vega
The text of this book was set in Bembo.

Printed in the United States of America
10 9 8 7 6 5 4 3 2 1

Library of Congress Control Number 2002115975

ISBN 0-689-84920-6

To my mother, Helen Heyes, whose story waits to be told

# CHAPTER ONE

"What we really need," Virginia said, "is a skeleton."

"Yeah," I said. "Let's just go get one. I think they're on sale at the A&P."

Am I a wit or what? Virginia rolled her eyes, like she always does. "Billy, you're clearly not taking this show seriously enough. How do you suggest we make the set look spooky?"

Calling it a "set" was sort of an exaggeration. We were in the tiny backyard of my auntie Annie's house, and we had decided our stage would be the area east of the clothesline. That would give us a way to hang a curtain, and there would be more room for our inevitably huge audience on the other side of the yard. See, Virginia and I are professional movie actors but are unemployed for the moment. We figured if we charged one-cent admission, we could make enough money to take ourselves to see *Tarzan the Ape Man*.

As I cast about the yard for set decoration ideas, Dad emerged from behind the garage dragging a couple of planks of wood. "How's these?" he asked, laying them on the scruffy grass.

Our play was going to be a ghost story with tap dancing, so we needed a wooden stage. We had written the script ourselves. Not bad for a couple of eleven-year-olds, huh?

Virginia stepped onto the boards and tried a couple of dance steps. She grinned at my dad, and he joined her and did a few steps of his own. Virginia's a pretty good dancer, but my dad is better.

"How about cobwebs?" I said, interrupting their little routine. "You think maybe we can make fake ones, Dad?"

He looked pleased at that idea. "You could go to one of the mills and ask for some scraps of cotton," he said. "They'd be tickled to have someone pick it up off the floor." He ruffled my hair, and I gave him a hug.

"We could stretch the cotton strands out in the corners of our set," Virginia said to me as Dad headed into the house. "Do you think that would work?"

"Sure," I said. "There's a mill a few blocks from here, on Nash Street. And we could set some old dusty things around, you know, for atmosphere."

"Not likely. Your aunt"—she glanced toward the house and lowered her voice—"your aunt is so nutty about cleanliness, I don't think we'd find anything with a speck of dust on it in this house."

"Well . . ." I knew I was asking for trouble. "There is a haunted house a few blocks from here. Maybe we could find something good in there."

"Haunted?"

I already wished I'd kept my mouth shut. Her eyes had a scary gleam in them. That's never good.

"Nah, it's not really haunted. Kids around here just call it that." I straightened my shoulders. "I don't believe in ghosts. It's just an abandoned house with weeds and vines and stuff growing all over it."

"Is it boarded up?"

"Uh-uh. It's like the owner just went out one day and never came back. He probably couldn't keep up his payments."

That kind of thing had happened to a lot of people in New Bedford lately. The mills started closing even before the stock market crashed in 1929. In the three years since the crash, still more mills had gone out of business, which of course meant people lost their jobs. Some people lost their houses to the bank, and some to the city because they couldn't pay their taxes.

My parents had moved in with Auntie Annie for sort of the same reason, except that instead of a regular house, they had been renting the downstairs half of a tenement on the next block. Virginia had looked horrified when I told her my family lived in a tenement. But "tenement" doesn't mean the same thing in New Bedford that it does in New York. Here, it's a house with one family living upstairs and another downstairs. Some tenements have three floors. Anyway, ours wasn't grand or anything, but we had the space we needed, and my parents had furniture of their own. When my dad lost his job six months ago my parents couldn't pay the rent, and the landlord evicted them. So now we're all stuffed into Auntie Annie's house.

Virginia and I grabbed our bikes, and I led the

way east toward Brooklawn Park. The North End isn't exactly the rich part of New Bedford, but Brooklawn is a nice park, with tennis courts, a little zoo, and a pond we would be able to skate on in winter—if we stayed here that long.

The house I was thinking of was different from most in the Brooklawn Park neighborhood. It was bigger, and it sat way back from the street. It had a low stone wall around the yard like the kind you see around houses that have been here since the Revolutionary War. This house didn't look that old, but it was obvious that no one had lifted a finger to take care of it in years. Azalea bushes were doing their best to bloom from underneath the tangle of vines that covered the yard. Vines also spiraled up the rain gutters to the roof, while shrubs that had probably looked pretty good in their day sprawled across the stone walkway and each other. A dusting of yellow-green pine pollen coated everything.

We stopped at the low iron gate in front of the house. A canopy of maple and oak leaves shaded the yard.

Virginia got off her bike and pushed open the gate. Now, I should have known the gate in front of an old haunted house would squeak—wouldn't you? But boy, did it make me jump. We propped the bikes against the wall. Suddenly I had a bad feeling. "Well," I said, "guess there's nothing here. Let's go back."

"It's perfect." She headed toward the house. Like a goof, I followed.

"It's probably locked," I said. "Let's go back."

Virginia whirled on me. "Billy O'Dwyer, this was your idea. You can't chicken out now. If you were brave enough to live with Maureen Fritz, you can manage to look around an abandoned house."

Maureen was my former manager, and she had been pretty scary, all right. I had to live with her in New York while I was making movies. See, that's how Virginia Grady and I met—we were supposed to make a series of pictures together about two kids called Rusty and Fred. But before filming could start, we got involved in a murder investigation at the studio, and things got complicated. An actress turned up dead, and my former costar and best pal Roscoe "Chubby" Muldoon almost had to take the rap for it. It's a long story, but the results were that the studio shut down, I moved back home with my parents, and Virginia ended up living here for a while too. And she sure knew where to dig when she wanted to talk me into doing something.

"All right, all right," I said.

We pushed our way through the brambles, stepping mostly in the places that were already smashed down. Apparently we weren't the first kids to come snooping around the house. We climbed the wooden steps to the piazza and found that, as I'd astutely predicted, the door was locked. Relieved, I turned to go. But something held me back: Virginia's grip on my suspenders.

"No, you don't," she said. "Let's try a window."

Next thing I knew, we were scrambling into the dark parlor of the old house. It smelled of dust, mildew, and mouse droppings. I was sure I heard the feet of creepy little creatures skittering around.

Virginia unlocked the front door, kicking aside some papers that lay on the floor. She wrestled the door open, and things brightened up enough for us to see our way around. It really did look as if whoever lived here had left in the middle of an ordinary day and never come back.

The parlor furniture was the kind that has little

claws for feet—a couple of faded red chairs beside a little table; a small, striped sofa with a low table in front of it; and another small table against the wall near the window. A desk sat opposite the window, its top rolled back to reveal a row of tiny drawers, a man's pipe, a few pens, a typewriter, and some scattered paper. A lamp with a gold-tasseled shade stood dustily on the table by the wall, but another lay broken on the floor in front of the chairs.

Virginia surveyed the room. "Look at all those scratches in the chairs. Cats," she speculated. "Well, there's plenty of dusty stuff here. Do you think it's all right for us to borrow some for our show?"

"Sure," I said. "Who would ever know? This guy's gone for good, whoever he was."

"I mean, we wouldn't really be stealing," she went on. "We'll bring it all back."

"Who's chickening out now?" I taunted.

"I'm not chickening out. I just don't like taking things that aren't mine."

She nudged the broken lamp with her foot, then stooped to pick up something from beneath it. It was a small brown book. She choked on dust as she

**EILEEN HEYES**

leafed through it. "Here's the guy's diary," she said. Her voice slipped into a deep, dramatic tone as she read from the book: "'They're all fools. They can rot, for all I care. I've got mine, I've got plenty. My house, my boat, my treasure. It's all I need.'"

"He sounds mean," I said.

"Or lonely." She kept turning pages. "Looks like he had a change of heart. 'I have been by myself long enough. I will face the changes, rejoin the world. All is ready.' This ends three years ago—June second, nineteen twenty-nine. That must be when he went away. I wonder why he left his diary behind?"

I began scouting around. With each step, I felt a sticky spiderweb clutch at some part of my body. "Gosh, I wish we could take these cobwebs with us. They'd be great. How about some of his books? They're good and dusty. Or that vase over there?"

"Listen to this," Virginia said. "He wrote a poem:

'Riches sweet, swelled with time.
My stock in trade, treasure is mine.
No one's to know, no one's to sea,

Rolling and cool, gold it shall be.
At grieving's end, a world to gain,
The greatest treasure man can know.
The answer to a sailor's pain
Awaits beyond the *Sunset's Glow.*'"

I took the diary from her and read the poem aloud, in the spookiest tone I could muster. "He can't spell," I said. "Sea should be s-e-e. See?"

"I wonder what happened to his treasure? What do you think it was?"

"Who knows? He probably just imagined it. Who's got treasure these days? Let's go look upstairs. I bet there's spooky stuff up there." I set the diary on the table and led the way, this time not at all caught off guard by the creaking of the stairs.

In the upstairs hall, we saw two closed doors and one that stood ajar. We headed for the open door. It led to a bedroom with a big, unmade four-poster between narrow windows that faced the backyard. The shades were half open, and we could see that animals or kids had been there. A washstand lay on its side, a broken basin and shards of mirror beside it. A walnut wardrobe lay facedown near the foot of the bed, held a few inches off the floor by something underneath it. The sheets and quilt looked like someone had tried to yank them off the bed; they were barely tucked under the mattress and were stretched across the floor and under the wardrobe.

"What a mess," I said, halting at the door. "I don't think there's anything in here we want."

But Virginia had already squeezed past me and was poking around inside the room, brushing aside spiderwebs as she went. "This is really strange," she said. "Why would anyone leave a house in this condition?"

"Props," I reminded her. "We're looking for props. It doesn't matter why it looks like this, and the place is starting to give me the creeps. Let's go back downstairs, grab a few things we can use, and get out of here."

She headed around the corner of the bed toward the window, stumbling on the sheet that had been pinned to the floor by the fallen wardrobe. "Yikes," she said, regaining her balance. "There's something under that sheet."

I bent to try to move the wardrobe. It was heavy, but I managed to wrench it up just enough for Virginia to pull the bedclothes free. As she did, something clunked against the floor.

We both stood up and screamed.

There, peeking out from beneath the big piece of furniture, was the hideously grinning head of a skeleton.

# CHAPTER TWO

We must have looked like a couple of those Keystone Kops from the silent movies, tripping over each other and banging into walls as we ran into the hall, down the stairs, and out the front door. We didn't stop until we were on the other side of the creaky front gate.

Virginia leaned on the stone wall, clutching her chest and panting, while I courageously . . . well, leaned on the wall, clutching my stomach and panting. "See?" I managed to say. "I told you it was haunted."

"That was no ghost," she said between gasps. "That was a dead body. Somebody bumped that guy off."

Virginia likes to talk in corny gangster slang like that. I think she's seen too many movies. "I bet they croaked him for his treasure," she continued.

"Jeez, that was creepy. Let's get out of here."

"I wonder if they ever found it?"

As my breathing settled down, I suddenly realized where this was leading. "Oh, no," I said. "Don't get ideas. We're calling the police."

"Police?" She gave me a blank look, like this was the furthest thing from her mind—which it probably was. "Oh, sure. Police. You're right. They should be the ones to investigate the murder."

I didn't like the sound of that. "And?"

"And we can find the missing treasure," she said, as if explaining the obvious to a dim-witted child.

"Uh-uh, not a chance."

"Billy, you know we did a great job on our last case."

"You mean when we almost got killed because of our brilliant deductions? That last case?"

"But the right guy got caught in the end, thanks to us. Remember?"

All I remembered was the terror I had felt when

I was sure we were going to die. "I'm not playing detective with you anymore," I said, climbing onto my bike.

As Virginia did the same, she looked at my bike, then at me, with eyebrows raised. "We wouldn't have these bikes if we hadn't been such smart detectives."

This was true. Roscoe Muldoon had sent these nifty bicycles to thank us for clearing his name. I'd seen a story about him in the newspaper just recently. He and some other big-name actors had gotten together and bought the studio where we all used to work.

"Yeah well, this time we're gonna be smart enough to leave it to the cops."

She got back off her bike. "Let's just take one more look around so we can give them a good description of the crime scene."

"You look," I said. "I'm not going in there again."

I thought I saw her mouth curl into a smile as she turned for the house. Watching her march through the front door we'd left open, I could only shake my head. Virginia sure can be stubborn.

Five minutes later, we were on our way back to

Auntie Annie's house. When we got there, we told my dad what we'd found, and he called the Weld Street police station. Then the three of us went back to the haunted house to wait. It wasn't nearly as scary with Dad there.

Before long, three cop cars came screaming up to the house with sirens blaring, like that pile of bones under the wardrobe was going to make a quick getaway if they didn't act fast. Almost before the first car had screeched to a halt at the curb, the driver jumped out and hustled over to my dad. "You Mr. O'Dwyer?" the cop asked.

"I am," Dad said.

"So where's this skeleton?" He cast an uneasy look toward the house. I was glad even a cop found the whole thing creepy.

"I'll show you," Virginia volunteered before Dad could answer. "I'm the one who found it." She stuck out her hand to the cop. "Virginia Grady."

It took him a moment to realize he was supposed to shake hands with her. But we young thespians are trained to be gracious and charming to adults, no matter what. Our careers can depend on it.

**EILEEN HEYES**

The cop peered at her, then at me. "You two look awfully familiar," he said.

"They're actors," Dad said. "You've probably seen Billy here in the movies."

"Oh, yeah," the cop said. "You're the kid from *Call Me Pop,* aren't you?" He eyed Virginia. "And you're the girl on the bike in the Baker's Chocolate ads, right?"

She nodded, smiling a well-trained smile. "*And* I'm the one who found the skeleton," she reminded him. "Want to see it?"

Acting as if making such a discovery were nothing unusual, Virginia led the cop through the bushy yard and told him our story. Dad and I followed, exchanging glances now and then when Virginia's narrative got particularly dramatic. I noticed she left out the part about how two petrified kids nearly crippled themselves stumbling down the stairs to flee a guy who was in no shape to hurt anyone. She also left out the part about the diary.

Pretty soon there were two other cops in the house with us, one of them carrying a camera. Flashbulbs popped as he took pictures of the room and the remains. It was almost an hour before they finally packed up their stuff and the dead guy. The first cop, whose name was Sergeant Ferreira, warned us not to disturb anything in the house as we followed the cops back through the parlor and across the yard.

Outside, a crowd had gathered on the sidewalk. There were grim-faced men, women in faded floral dresses, and wide-eyed kids cowering behind the grown-ups. A few of the men wore the ragged, dirty clothes that marked them as hoboes—guys who followed the railroad tracks in search of work. One held a little dog under his arm. Another, whose shirt was actually pretty clean, wore a hat like a train engineer's. For people who would have trouble even paying the nickel it cost to see a movie, the spectacle of a skeleton being taken from a haunted house was fine entertainment.

That evening after supper, I pulled out a deck of cards for our usual Friday night whist game. We had taught Virginia how to play, and she'd gotten pretty good. Whenever Auntie Annie didn't feel like playing, which was often, Virginia teamed with my mom. As I started shuffling the cards, I was surprised to see Virginia come downstairs in a dress instead of her overalls. Before I had a chance to question her, my dad appeared behind her wearing his only suit.

"What's going on?" I asked.

Dad cleared his throat. "We'll explain it to you later, all right?"

I nodded, feeling something like envy give me a little poke in the stomach. Dad ruffled my hair, and they headed out the door.

"Mom," I called. "Hey, Mom."

"In here."

I put down the cards and followed the voice into the kitchen, where my mom was drying dishes. My little sister, Olive, sat on the floor dressing her two favorite dolls. Mom handed me a plate, and I put it into the cupboard.

"Where are Dad and Virginia going all dressed up?" I asked.

"He's taking her to Tiferes Israel." She pushed a brown curl off her forehead with the back of her wrist. "Friday night services. It's the beginning of her Sabbath, you know."

I knew Virginia was Jewish, because her mom was

and that's the way it works with Jewish people. "But she's never wanted to go to a Sabbath service before," I said.

"Well, she wanted to go tonight. Here, this is the last of them, thank goodness." She handed me Auntie Annie's big stew pot and hung the dish towel to dry. The pot was still damp, but I put it in the drawer without pointing that out. Mom did most of the cooking and all the kitchen cleaning, tasks that did not fill her with joy.

"Olive," Mom said. "Pick up them doll things."

My sister grabbed one naked doll and its dress and followed me and Mom back into the parlor. Auntie Annie came down the stairs and disappeared into the kitchen without a word to any of us. She's like that sometimes.

Olive plopped onto the couch while Mom made her usual circuit around the room picking things up, setting them on shelves, or dropping them into her apron pockets to take upstairs. "Can't you two put your things away like Virginia does? If I hear Annie moaning one more time about—"

"Ivy! What's this mess in here?"

Mom stiffened and looked at Olive, who slid off

the couch and scurried into the kitchen. "I told her to pick up them things," Mom muttered.

The three of us spent the next few hours hiding out upstairs, reading. At last, right after Mom had put Olive to bed, we heard Dad's Whippet pull up to the garage.

Mom and I met them at the door. Auntie Annie was in the parlor knitting, so the rest of us settled in the kitchen and Mom made tea.

"You see, Billy," Dad said, "Virginia's been missing her parents since her aunt—"

"Unloaded me on you," Virginia interrupted.

"Now, Virginia," Dad said.

"Well, it's true. She could hardly wait to get rid of me."

Virginia had come home with me for what we thought would be a short visit, right after we solved our murder case at the studio. But that had been two months ago. Almost immediately, letters and phone calls had started arriving from the aunt she was living with in New York and from her parents, who were in Germany because her father was teaching at a university there. Next thing I knew, my dad announced that he had become Virginia's guardian and we should consider her part of our family. This did not sit well with Dad's sister, who already thought there were too many people living in her house. But my dad was out of work, and Virginia's father started sending money to cover her room and board, so Auntie Annie stopped complaining quite so loudly.

"Virginia's mum always took her to synagogue," Dad was explaining, "and she wanted to start going again. She hasn't been in a long time."

"Your aunt didn't—?" I began.

"Aunt Trudi's not Jewish," Virginia said. "She's always hated my mom. The only reason she took me in was that she needed my father's money."

Finally I understood why Virginia was still with us. She had no place else to go. I was glad when Mom said the very mushy thing I was thinking.

"We're happy to have you, Virginia. You're always welcome here."

After breakfast the next morning, I foolishly let Virginia talk me into checking out our bone guy. Not that I had any intention of investigating anything, no sirree. I just wanted to know if they'd figured out who he was and how he was killed. After that, it would absolutely be a police matter. No more face-to-face encounters with killers for me.

Of course, Virginia simply rolled her eyes when I told her this.

We rode our bikes down Ashley Boulevard to the police station, which was about a mile from my house. We had dressed a lot like Rusty and Fred, the characters we had almost played in those movies that ended up not getting made. I wore knickers and suspenders, and Virginia braided her hair and wore her tomboy overalls. I even put on my newsboy cap, and Virginia popped a baseball cap onto her head. I don't know why, but we both felt like we could handle adults better when we were in costume.

"Hiya," I said to the watch commander as we strode maturely up to the front desk.

He looked up and grunted. "Yeah?"

"We're here about the skeleton from the Brooklawn house," Virginia said. "What have you found out about the guy? Do you think he was killed by the Mob?"

As might have been predicted, the watch commander was not eager to share police business with a couple of kids—even perky, charismatic kids like us.

"The Mob?" He looked amused. "Why don't you kids just go home? This is none of your concern."

At that moment, I saw Sergeant Ferreira come out from a back room.

"Hiya, Sergeant Ferreira," I called. "How's it going?"

He came over. "Well, well. Have you kids recovered from your fright yesterday?" To the watch commander's puzzled look, Ferreira said, "These are the kids who found that skeleton. Gave 'em a good scare, eh?"

"We were wondering if you had found out why the poor man was killed," Virginia said.

"Step into my office."

We followed him, exchanging surprised glances. Despite Virginia's confidence, I don't think either of us expected it to be that easy. What Ferreira called his office was actually just a desk at the back of the cramped little station. He motioned us to pull over a couple of chairs and sit.

"There's not much to tell," he said. "The poor man wasn't killed. And he wasn't all that poor, either. Not in the usual way."

"Who was he?" Virginia asked.

"His name was John Frederick Wilkinson. That was his house. Lived in New Bedford all his life."

"What happened to him?" I said.

"It looks like he somehow pulled the wardrobe over on himself," Ferreira said.

We waited for more. I'd learned this trick from Virginia: Sometimes if you just keep your mouth shut, people will tell you all kinds of things you couldn't have dragged out of them with questions.

"We figure he was tugging on that bedsheet trying to get himself free but couldn't do it," Ferreira went on, "and after a while he just died there. Our best guess is that he's been lying there for a few years. Imagine." He shook his head.

I frowned, trying to make sense of this, but Virginia understood immediately. "No one missed him," she said.

"Nope," Ferreira said. "Apparently not."

"Wait a minute," I said. "How could a guy not come out of his house for three years and no one miss him?"

"Think about it, Billy," Virginia said. "Who would miss *you?* Your family, your chums—anyone who expected you to be somewhere, right? Mr.

Wilkinson must not have had any of that."

Ferreira nodded.

"That's what you meant," Virginia said, her voice quiet with sadness, "about him not being poor in the usual way?"

"That's right. We're going to run an obituary for him in the *Evening Standard* and the *Boston Globe*. We know he had a son who moved to Boston some years ago, so maybe he'll see the obit and come back."

"If he didn't care enough to see his dad when he was alive, why would he come back now?" Virginia asked.

"He stands to inherit that big house free and clear, except for some back taxes. Mr. Wilkinson might have had some money, too. We're looking into that. The son could inherit a small fortune."

I considered this legacy. "A house, a bunch of money, and no dad," I said. "Some inheritance."

# CHAPTER THREE

That afternoon, we rode our bikes back to the Wilkinson house. It looked even more forlorn, though nothing had changed since the day before. The front door remained closed, as the police had left it. The pair of windows in the attic gable gazed out at the street like close-set drowsy eyes, with shades pulled halfway down and the darkness of death behind the lower panes.

I shivered in the mid-June sunshine as we leaned on the cool stone wall and studied the house.

"It's a nice house," Virginia said. "I mean, it must have been, sometime back. This guy was rich. A big house, a boat, his treasure—whatever it is."

"Was," I corrected. "Whatever it was, it's probably

long gone. And we are not going to look for it. Okay? He was just a sad, old guy who had an accident in his house and died from it. There's nothing to investigate, Sherlock. Case closed."

"Sad is right," she said. "He must have lived alone for a long time. I wonder why the son never came to see him?"

"I can answer that."

Virginia and I jumped at the sound of the voice behind us. A guy in ragged clothes stood on the sidewalk a few feet from us, twisting a cloth cap in his hands. Unlike most hoboes, he looked like he had shaved recently, and his shirt was pretty clean. It took me a second to place him. Then I remembered: He'd been in the crowd watching the cops take away John Wilkinson's remains. He pushed his engineer cap into a pocket of his baggy work pants and ran his hand over his hair, straightening it.

"You knew the family?" Virginia asked.

"Knew them?" He barked out a little laugh. "Yeah, I knew them. I was practically one of them." He sat on the stone wall. "John Wilkinson was like a second father to me when I was growing up. He used to help me with my schoolwork, pay me to do little jobs around here or on his boat. Used to have me over for dinner all the time, especially after his wife died."

"When was that?" I said.

"Long time ago. She died when J. J. and I were kids. J. J.'s the son." He seemed to suddenly remember his manners. "My name's Eddie Talbott. You're the kids who found Mr. Wilkinson, aren't you?"

"Virginia Grady." She stuck out her hand, as always. The Talbott guy shook it for a long time and looked at her like she was his long-lost friend or something. A flush rose in her cheeks.

"Sorry, I don't mean to stare," he said. "Those gorgeous eyes of yours—they remind me of the girl I was in love with in high school."

She threw me a flustered look, then stammered, "And, um, this is Billy O'Dwyer."

All I got was a quick, manly shake.

"Mr. Talbott, when was the last time you saw Mr. Wilkinson?" Virginia asked, her usual composed and lawyerlike self again.

"Just Eddie, please. It was years ago. I left town for a while, and we kind of lost touch. Is it true that when you found him, he was . . ." His voice trailed off.

"A skeleton," I said, nodding. I filled him in on what Sergeant Ferreira had said.

"And he just lay there hurt until he died?" Eddie put his head down, a hand covering his eyes. After a moment, he lifted his head and said haltingly, "He was in there all that time. If only I'd tried to see him. If only I'd known. It's like—like losing my own father again." He took a deep, ragged breath. "Mr. Wilkinson was a great man. A talented man. He played the clarinet. Did you know that? And wrote poetry. He didn't show it to very many people, but he used to show me, to encourage me to keep reading and working hard in school. He'd have me copy his poems to practice my penmanship."

"We found one of his poems," Virginia said. "He must have written it not too long before he died."

"You did? What was it about? Or couldn't you tell? He had such a brilliant mind, I couldn't always follow what he was trying to say."

"Yeah," I said. "This was one of those." I recited the poem from the diary.

"Say it again," Eddie said. He made me go through it two more times, while he repeated the lines. Then he nodded. "Yup, that's John Wilkinson for you. Dreaming of gold, looking out past the sun-set. That's exactly the kind of guy he was." He pushed himself off the wall. "Well, I'd better be going. You kids live around here?"

"Over near Abe Lincoln School," I said. "On Glennon Street."

"Oh sure, I know that neighborhood. And hey, thanks for what you've done. You know, finding Mr. Wilkinson, so he can maybe at least have a decent burial. And thanks for telling me about the poem. His words mean a lot to me, more than you know."

"Anytime," Virginia said, smiling a little more than I thought was necessary. She waved as he headed off down the street, then turned to me. "How did you remember that whole poem? You only saw it once."

"It wasn't that long," I said. She waited for more, the way she always does. "Maureen used to smack me around if I ever forgot a line. Even if it was just at rehearsal, she wanted me to have every line down perfect. So I learned to memorize real fast."

"Billy O'Dwyer, you are a person with many hidden talents."

"Yeah," I agreed modestly. "But I still don't know what the poem means."

"Maybe we can get some clues from Eddie." She patted my shoulder reassuringly. "Don't worry. We'll figure it out."

That was what I was afraid of.

To my great relief, the rest of the day went by without her mentioning this pointless investigation in which I was not going to participate. We spent the afternoon helping my dad bottle his homemade beer to take to his buddies from the Workingman's Club. Don't worry—he has legal permission to make it, Prohibition or no Prohibition. And if the guys at his club are willing to give him a little cash for the stuff, well, is that a crime? Okay, yeah, maybe the law says it is a crime. But it's not that much beer, or that much money, and—like Dad says all the time—hardly anyone really pays attention to the Volstead Act.

Except maybe the poor stiffs in the Coast Guard. There'd been a front-page story in the *Evening Standard* the day before about them catching another rumrunner. Dad's a big newspaper reader, and this story sent him on one of his rants about how incompetently the government was being run.

"They're wasting their time," Dad had said.

"There's more whiskey on them ships out there than these buggers will ever stop coming in. And what's the use? The people are going to get their whiskey, whatever it takes. Trying to stop them—it's just making money for the crooks."

I had read every word of the story. The ships bring all this booze from Scotland or someplace and then they sit about twenty miles offshore where the Coast Guard isn't allowed to bother them. Some local people take their boats out at night and load up with whiskey and then sneak it ashore. They're the ones the Coast Guard chases.

I wondered why Dad got more hot under the collar about rumrunners than he'd gotten when I told him that Maureen had been beating me for two years. Sure, he'd listened, and he had promised never to send me back to her. But the only time he'd mentioned it again was after his brother Bob in New York agreed to take me in if I went back to make more movies.

Anyway, see, it was turning out to be a normal Saturday, and I figured Virginia had come to her senses and we could get on with our show.

I figured wrong.

The next day, around noon, when she and I were sitting on the front piazza listening to our stomachs growl, a former New York cop named Jimmy Mandell showed up. Jimmy had been involved in our murder investigation at the studio. He hadn't exactly been an honest cop, and had a fancy gold ring and some other expensive stuff to show for it. But his conscience had finally gotten to him, and when that case was over, he'd quit the police force. He'd moved back home with his parents, who lived in Fall River, which is real close to New Bedford.

Jimmy was a big guy, about a foot taller than my dad. He'd been pretty beefy when he was in New York, but he'd lost some of that bulk in his two months back home. I wondered whether his mom was a lousy cook or he was actually trying to lose weight. He'd also quit wearing the gold ring.

Jimmy had been to dinner at Auntie Annie's house a couple of times. My parents had insisted, because they were grateful to him for helping me and Virginia when we'd gotten ourselves into trouble. But his appearance this Sunday was a surprise.

Even more surprising to us was that, just as Jimmy stepped up onto the piazza, Auntie Annie burst through the front door to greet him. She was wearing what my mom calls a church dress—the kind she'd wear to church, if she ever went—and a string of pearls around her neck. I even caught a whiff of some flowery perfume. Virginia, who was sitting in the high-backed rocking chair reading a library book called *The Secret of the Old Clock,* watched Auntie Annie and then shot me a look. I shrugged. Auntie Annie can be pretty strange.

"Why, Jimmy," she gushed. "Come in, come in. It's so nice of you to join us again for dinner."

"Thanks, ma'am," Jimmy said. "Hi, kids. How are you doing?"

"Great, Jimmy," I said. "How about you?"

Before Jimmy could answer, Auntie Annie hustled him into the parlor, the smells of a hot, meat-and-potatoes dinner streaming out the door to fill the space Jimmy had occupied on the piazza.

Virginia scowled. "She must be ten years older than he is," she said with a cluck of disapproval, then turned back to her book.

Fifteen long, hungry minutes later, we all sat at the table with plates of beef and kidney pie, steaming cabbage, and sliced bread in front of us. Virginia ate the chunks of kidney from her plate first, trying to disguise her disgust. I had to admit, the girl had guts. Me, I just pushed my portion of kidneys aside, hoping to get out of eating them altogether. Olive was more blunt, plucking each ugly little gray kidney bit from her plate and dropping it onto my mom's. You can get away with that kind of stuff when you're three.

Under Auntie Annie's questioning, Jimmy was going on about his career plans.

"So I got myself a comparison microscope," he said, "and a good camera, and I set up a darkroom in my folks' garage. I already know plenty about examining documents and handwriting, from when I was in New York. I figure I can get work as a detective." He glanced at me and Virginia. "Good, honest work."

Virginia and I exchanged a look. We both knew perfectly well that Jimmy hadn't bought that stuff with money he'd made through good, honest work.

"What exactly is that equipment for?" Dad asked.

"Analyzing crime scenes, Mr. O'Dwyer," Jimmy said. "See—"

"Oh, you can call him Bill," Auntie Annie interrupted.

Jimmy paused, looking from her to my dad. "Yeah. Well, this microscope lets me put two samples side by side—like hair, or blood, or bullets—and see if they match up. You can identify bad guys that way, or tell if a certain gun fired a certain bullet. And the camera—"

"Is for taking pictures of bodies," Virginia put in. "Right?" She had that scary gleam in her eyes again.

Jimmy laughed. I thought he was being awfully patient, considering no one seemed willing to let him finish a sentence.

"Yes miss, sometimes bodies. Or sometimes just the place itself. You can tell a lot from things like footprints, or how branches are broken, or which way the furniture is facing. So you kids are still interested in solving crimes?"

"No," I said firmly.

"Sure," Virginia chirped. "In fact, we're working on a new case right now."

And off she went, telling Jimmy all about the skeleton and the police and the friend of the dead guy. She got so carried away with her story that she even spilled the part about the diary and the treasure.

"A crazy poem and a mysterious missing treasure, eh?" Jimmy laughed again, shaking his head.

"You two are gonna be like them kids—what are they called? The Hardy Boys."

Virginia beamed. I groaned. Olive clapped her fat little hands.

Auntie Annie had apparently had enough of this line of conversation. She got up, pushed her chair back, and said, "Jimmy, why don't you come relax out on the piazza. Our Ivy will clean up when the children have finished, won't you then?" She cast my mom a smile with all the sincerity of a chorus girl looking for work.

Mom stared at her. "Of course, Annie."

"Thanks, love," Auntie Annie said, and she guided Jimmy away from the table and out the front door.

"I'll do it," Virginia said swiftly. She leaped out of her chair, and before I knew it had scooped up her plate and fork from the table along with mine and Olive's and vanished into the kitchen.

That kid is a born rescuer. She had gotten me out of awkward, even dangerous, situations before, but nothing quite like this. This time, she'd saved me from having to eat those revolting hunks of kidney.

I knew right then that Virginia would be my friend for life.

# CHAPTER FOUR

Just like Ferreira said, John Wilkinson's obituary appeared in the *New Bedford Evening Standard* that Monday. It was pretty short. What was there to say? The guy was found dead in his home, apparently of natural causes. Memorial services had not yet been planned.

I remembered Eddie's comment about Wilkinson getting a proper burial, and wondered who might arrange that for a guy with no family in town.

Virginia and I had taken to riding over to the house every day, just to look at it. We had abandoned the idea of getting anything out of it to use in our show. She seemed to have abandoned the show itself, but I still wanted to put it on. This was the last week of school, so we would have plenty of kids available soon to be our audience. Besides, I was looking forward to seeing my old pals again. Even though Abe Lincoln School was just up the street, my dad hadn't bothered enrolling us, because we had come to town so late in the year.

When we pulled up to the Wilkinson place on Tuesday, Virginia said, "Let's go inside and look around one more time."

"For what? Another skeleton?"

"For clues to the treasure, of course. We're running out of time. If the son shows up, we won't get another chance."

That would have been fine with me. I was ready for this case to be over. We parked the bikes, and I followed her into the bushy yard, muttering my misgivings. I think we both heard the noise at the same time. We froze.

"What was that?" She looked toward the far corner of the piazza, where the sound had come from. "Quick, hide."

We tucked ourselves as far down into the brambles as we could and watched the bushes on the side of the house quiver. Then Eddie Talbott emerged from the green shadows, looking toward the upstairs windows, and we began to breathe again.

Virginia leaped to her feet. "Eddie," she called.

He turned, a look of panic on his face. For a second I thought he was going to bolt. But then his face relaxed, and he started picking his way through the overgrown yard toward us.

"Hi, kids," he said. "I was just taking a look around." We followed him as he continued through the yard and out the gate. He sat on the cool stone wall. "Can't see much through the windows. Too dark inside."

We all looked at one another and the house for a minute in awkward wordlessness. But what broke the silence was even more uncomfortable.

A car pulled up across the street, and a guy in a gray pinstripe suit stepped out and strode toward us. He was shorter and stouter than Eddie, with dark, heavy eyebrows that made him look a little like a werewolf.

Eddie's whole attitude changed. He stood, and I could see his jaw muscles tighten and his fingers start to curve.

"Talbott," the stranger said, stopping a few feet away. "What are you doing here?"

"I could ask you the same thing," Eddie snarled.

"I came to see about my father." He stepped up onto the granite curb. "As if you didn't know."

Eddie smirked. "You just missed him. By about three years."

The other man recoiled as if he'd been slapped. "Get off this property." He took a step toward Eddie, not seeming to notice Virginia and me at all. "Or I'll have the cops haul you off it."

"This is a public sidewalk, J. J. I have just as much right to be here as you do. Maybe more."

The stranger sucked in his breath, his right shoulder cocking back a bit. I thought he was going to slug Eddie. Instead, he turned and stalked back to his car. In an instant he was gone, leaving a cloud of fury and car exhaust hanging over the street.

Eddie let out a sigh. "So," he said after a moment. "Now you've met Mr. Wilkinson's son. Nice guy, huh?"

"Wow," I said. "He looks pretty dangerous."

"Why was he so angry at you?" Virginia asked. "I thought you and J. J. grew up together."

"We did." He gazed down the street, in the direction that J. J.'s car had driven off. "We used to do everything together. Like brothers. The other rich kids at school used to tease him because he hung around with me, the son of a handyman." He let out a little chuckle, as if that young J. J. was someone he remembered warmly, some completely different person from the one we'd just seen. "He never listened to those snobs, though. J. J. always stuck up for me. And I stood up for him too. We sure got into some scrapes together."

He looked back at the house, that hint of a smile still on his face. I could tell he was enjoying the memory of his good times with this rich kid.

"Well, what happened?" I said.

Eddie looked at us for a few seconds, like he was trying to decide where to begin. Finally he said, "Well, there was the girl I told you about— the one with eyes like yours. We both fell for her." He paused, letting Virginia turn an annoying shade of pink while he gazed at her. Jeez. "And we also had different friends in high school. We quit doing things together. Then he left. I guess he just figured he'd gotten too fine to stay in a grubby mill town like New Bedford."

"Seems like his dad was doing pretty well here," I pointed out.

"Well enough to send J. J. to Harvard to get the education his father never had. Mr. Wilkinson taught himself everything—just like me. Always reading, always writing. But J. J. had the fancy college degree, so of course he thought that made him better than the rest of us. He decided to stay in Boston, near his Harvard pals."

"Boston's not that far," Virginia said. "Mr. Wilkinson should have been proud of his son making his way in a big city."

"He might have been," Eddie said, "if his son hadn't disowned him."

"How?" I asked.

"I don't know the full story. I think J. J. just told his father to stay out of his life. Mr. Wilkinson was a proud man. He never would have begged for anything. So when J. J. turned his back on him, Mr. Wilkinson let him go."

This whole conversation was making me uneasy. Fathers and sons shouldn't be turning their backs on each other. It wasn't natural. Every father needed a son and, for crying out loud, every son needed a father.

"Billy," I heard Virginia saying. "What's the matter?"

I realized I had tears running down my cheeks. "Nothing," I said, swiftly wiping my face. "Nothing. It's sad, that's all."

"Don't waste your tears," Eddie said. "J. J.'s not worth it. He's nothing but a stuck-up rich kid who's slumming now to collect his father's big house."

"And boat?" Virginia asked.

"Boat?" Eddie seemed surprised. "Oh, sure. I told you about the boat, didn't I? I used to work on it for Mr. Wilkinson. I don't know what ever happened to the boat."

"What kind of boat was it?" Virginia asked.

I had the feeling she was just making conversation while I got myself under control. She does that kind of stuff.

"A nice one," Eddie said. "It had lots of polished wood inside and out, real luxurious. We used to go deep-sea fishing on it. Mr. Wilkinson stopped using the boat after J. J. left. I tried to get him to take me fishing again, to cheer him up some. But he was heartbroken about the way his stuck-up son was treating him."

"Sounds like a real pretty boat," I said, feeling mostly normal again.

"It was beautiful," Eddie said. He snapped his fingers. "Would you like to see it? Mr. Wilkinson had a painting of it in his room."

Virginia and I looked at each other. I didn't mind sitting out here at the stone wall, but I wasn't in any hurry to go back into that spooky, smelly house.

"Sure," she said, of course.

We followed Eddie through the tangle of plants and onto the piazza. He tried the door, but it was locked.

"Eddie." She touched his arm, and even in the shadows I could see her blushing again. "We can try the window over here." She led him to the window we had climbed through the week before. He hoisted it open.

Although it was dim inside the house, I could see that everything was the way we'd left it Friday. Well, almost everything: Someone had moved the diary from where I'd left it on the little table.

"I don't think we ought to be in here," I said.

"It's okay," Eddie said, while we all waited for our eyes to adjust to the lack of light. "This is like coming home for me."

And he did seem pretty comfortable. He led the way up the stairs and into the room at the end of the hall. The room where that bony dead face had sneered up at us from the floor. I shivered.

Eddie halted at the door. "Is this where . . . ?"

"Yeah," I said. "This is where."

We all stood rooted for a moment. The cops hadn't tidied up this room much, but they'd at least set the wardrobe upright. When we walked in and looked at the painting opposite the foot of the bed, I could vaguely recall having seen it the day we'd been there before.

It showed ocean waves and a sunset—not exactly an unusual subject for an oil painting. Auntie Annie had something similar in her parlor, only smaller. But this one also had a long, sleek boat in it. The boat didn't seem to belong in the picture, but I wasn't sure why.

"How strange," Virginia said, "that the boat

looks this way. I mean, like there's a light shining on it. With the sun setting behind it, the boat should have been a silhouette."

"Yeah," Eddie said. "He loved that boat so much, he hired a guy to paint it in on top of this old picture."

"Who are the two people on the deck?" Virginia asked.

"Oh, that's us," Eddie said. "Mr. Wilkinson and me." He looked at us and added hastily, "or J. J. Probably Mr. Wilkinson and J. J." He gave a self-conscious little chuckle. "I never thought about it."

*Sure you didn't,* I thought. *Not a very convincing performance.*

He turned and headed out, calling over his shoulder, "Come on, kids, we'd better get out of here."

This time, instead of leaving us at the gate, Eddie waited until we'd gotten on our bikes and started toward home. As I rode, I glanced back and saw Eddie walking away in the other direction.

I don't know why, but I felt relieved to see him leaving John Wilkinson's house. And for some reason, I wished he would just keep going.

**EILEEN HEYES**

# CHAPTER FIVE

That afternoon, we rode the streetcar downtown so Virginia could return her book to the Free Public Library, which was one of her favorite places in town. She had loved the old building the minute she saw it, especially the statue out front of the guy in the whaling boat. The man is about to throw a harpoon at a whale, and the inscription says: A DEAD WHALE OR A STOVE BOAT. See, New Bedford was a big whaling town way before I was born and before the cotton mills got going. You can read about it in that book *Moby Dick*.

It's a long book, but my dad read me the chapters in the beginning about New Bedford and a lot of other good parts. The funny thing was, Virginia's mom had done the same thing with her. That's why she liked the statue right away.

She checked out another mystery and we left the library, heading for our streetcar stop.

"Uh-oh," she said. "Look who's here."

Across William Street, coming out of city hall, I saw J. J. Wilkinson. His felt hat shadowed most of his face, but I recognized the confident way he carried himself as he walked down the city hall steps. Like a stuck-up Harvard guy. He was looking at a piece of paper in his hands.

"It's about the treasure," Virginia said. "Whatever he's reading, it's about the treasure."

I wasn't going to argue. Instead, without knowing why, I took off trotting across the street. "Hiya, Mr. Wilkinson," I called, waving to him.

He cocked his head and peered at me with narrowed eyes. Stopping in front of him at the bottom of the steps, I gulped. He still looked dangerous.

"Hiya," I said again. "I'm Billy O'Dwyer." By habit, I stuck out my hand. He responded with an automatic shake, his face softening a little.

"Jacob Wilkinson. Do I know you?"

I was surprised by the gentleness in his voice, after

that scene in the North End a couple of hours earlier.

"Well no, not exactly. You might have seen me in the movies. *Call Me Pop*?"

He shook his head and shrugged.

"And I was with Eddie Talbott a little while ago when you stopped at your dad's house. . . ."

His face hardened again. By this time, Virginia had joined us.

"Oh," he said. "You're friends of Eddie's?"

"No, no," Virginia put in quickly. "We're the ones who found your father last week. Virginia Grady." Another handshake. "We just went to look at the house today and Eddie was there."

"Mr. Wilkinson, we're real sorry about your dad," I thought to say.

The kindness returned to his werewolf face. He even looked a little relieved. "Thank you," he said. "Did you . . . know my father?"

"No," I said. I wasn't sure where to go from here—tell him we broke into his dad's house looking for something as dumb as dusty books?

"We thought the house was abandoned," Virginia said, rescuing me as usual. She explained our plans for the show and made it sound pretty reasonable that a couple of kids would climb through a window and snoop around someone's old house.

He considered this for a moment, then actually threw back his head and laughed. "I'm sorry," he said, quieting down. "A ghost story with tap dancing. That's pretty original. I just . . . I shouldn't have laughed. I'm just. . . . I can't quite get used to what happened to my father." His face was fully serious again.

Then I did something very Virginia-like.

"When was the last time you saw your dad?" I asked. *That didn't come out right,* I thought. *I sound like a cop.*

But if J. J.—*Jacob*—Wilkinson thought I was out of line, he didn't show it. He sat down on a step, in that nice pinstripe suit, and took off his hat. "About six years ago," he said. "Right after I got married."

I sat next to him, and Virginia settled down on the other side of me. I gave him that sympathetic look I'd learned from her, the one that always gets people talking to us about stuff that's really none of our business.

"I brought my wife, Carmen, home to meet him. He'd missed our wedding."

"Why?" I said.

He hesitated, then said, "He refused to come. But I thought that once he met her he would accept her into the family."

"And he didn't?" I asked.

"No. Her family is Italian and Catholic, and that's all he needed to know. He threw us both out of his house. He had threatened to write me out of his will if I married her. In fact, he was always threatening that for one reason or another. I didn't need his money, though."

"He'd already put you through Harvard," I supplied.

He looked surprised. "How did you—? Oh. Talbott must have told you. Anyway, I was making good money. All I really wanted was for him to be proud of me and to accept the woman I chose for my wife."

"Do you have kids?" I didn't know why I was interviewing him like this, but I couldn't stop myself.

"Two of them," he said. "A two-year-old boy and a baby girl."

"And you never gave your father a chance to see his grandchildren?" Virginia's voice sounded almost accusing, but Mr. Wilkinson didn't seem to notice.

"I tried to get my father to accept them, too," he said. "I wrote to him and sent pictures, but he never responded. He had completely cut me off." He stopped abruptly and frowned.

"Did you say your son is two?" I asked.

Mr. Wilkinson looked at me, raising his bushy brows as he did the math. "I've just been in there"— he tilted his head toward city hall—"seeing about my father's property taxes and unpaid bills. It appears he died around the middle of nineteen twenty-nine."

I nodded.

"So he never knew," Mr. Wilkinson said. "He never knew he had grandchildren."

When we told him we were planning to take a street-car back to the North End, Mr. Wilkinson offered us a ride. He said he was on his way there to visit his dad's house, anyway. A few minutes later he pulled up in front of the Weld Street police station. "I have to stop here first and get the key from Sergeant Ferreira," he said, getting out of the car. We climbed out too.

"I'll be out in a minute. You two can wait here."

As Mr. Wilkinson walked away, Virginia mused quietly, "Yes, we *could* wait here—"

"But we're not going to, are we?" I said. She shook her head. Once he'd gone into the station, we sauntered up to the door, slipped in, and settled ourselves inconspicuously into a couple of chairs near the door.

Mr. Wilkinson had his back to us, but we could see that Sergeant Ferreira wore a look of grim satisfaction.

"Well, you see," he was saying, "I can't give you the key. A guy named Talbott came in a while ago waving a will and saying the house was his."

"What?" Mr. Wilkinson stepped halfway around the desk, showing us his werewolf profile. "A will? My father's will?"

"That's what it was. I had a good look at it. It was all typed up and signed by John Frederick Wilkinson."

"So you gave him the key?" Jacob Wilkinson's voice was rising, along with the color in his face.

"No. He didn't have all the paperwork quite right. I told him he'd have to get that will certified at the courthouse to make it legal, and then he could take possession of the property."

"Take possession of *my* father's house?" Mr. Wilkinson had that dangerous look again, the one that had scared me the first time we saw him. "The will's a fake. My father wouldn't leave his house to that gold digger Eddie Talbott. That house belongs to me."

"You'll have to take that up in court." Sergeant Ferreira's stiff posture and firm voice made it clear he wasn't buying Jacob Wilkinson's story. "I'm not a lawyer, but I'd guess you'd better have some kind of proof if you expect to invalidate that will. It looked real to me." He stood up. "Now, if you'll excuse me." Mr. Wilkinson stalked out into the sunshine, with us at his heels.

"The signature," Mr. Wilkinson said, nodding absently. "That'll show it's a fake."

"The signature compared with what?" Virginia said.

He snapped his head around, like he hadn't noticed we were there. "As it happens," he said, "I brought an old letter from my father, the last one he sent me."

"Strange coincidence," Virginia commented

ever so casually. I caught the insinuation in her voice, but Mr. Wilkinson didn't react to it.

"Oh, it's no coincidence. I always carry it." He paused. "Well, let me drive you kids home. I need to get to work on this before I lose my father's house."

I was about to accept, but Virginia said, "Thanks, but we can walk. It's not far." She pulled me away as I said a quick good-bye.

"Jeez," I said after half a block. "What's the matter with you?"

"I don't like him. He's going to try to cheat Eddie out of his inheritance."

I was stunned. "'Cheat Eddie'? Looks to me like Eddie's the one trying to cheat Jacob."

"Eddie was like a son to John Wilkinson. Jacob walked out on him. Who would you leave the house to if it were yours?"

I clenched my teeth. For some reason, the question made me angry. "I wouldn't leave it to a stranger," I said. "I wouldn't leave it to someone who tried to horn in on my family. I'd leave it to my own son."

# CHAPTER SIX

"Now let me get this straight." I was following Virginia down the sidewalk, away from Auntie Annie's house, the next day. "We're going to the police station."

"Obviously."

"And we're going to tell the police to call Jimmy Mandell . . ."

"Yes."

"And hire him to examine these documents . . ."

"The will and the letter, if there really is a letter."

"So they can solve something that's not even a crime . . ."

"Yup."

"And just because two kids strolled in and told them to, the cops are going to do this?"

She stopped and faced me. "Well, it works for Nancy Drew!"

"Who?"

"Never mind. Yes Billy, you have the picture now. That's exactly what we're going to do."

She had been distinctly snippy toward me since we'd met Jacob Wilkinson the day before. Not that I was feeling all warm and cozy about her, either. I couldn't imagine how she could believe Eddie and doubt Jacob. Sure, Jacob was kind of a hothead. Big deal. So is my dad, if you want the truth. That's why, the whole time I was living with Maureen, I hadn't told him that she was hitting me. I was sure that if he knew, he'd kill her. And maybe—okay, probably—Jacob could get violent when he was angry. But he was still John Wilkinson's son, and that's what mattered.

Virginia and I walked the rest of the way to the Weld Street police station without talking. When we got there, she marched right up to Ferreira's desk. "Sergeant," she said.

He looked up. "Oh, hi kids. How are you two doing? Find any more bodies today?" He actually chuckled, as if decomposed corpses were funny.

My partner, however, was all business. "This is not a laughing matter, Sergeant Ferreira," she said. "We came because we know just the man who can help you crack the Wilkinson case."

Ferreira put his head down and rubbed his forehead, like he had a headache or something. I wished I'd stayed home. When he raised his head again, he looked tired. "I told you kids before. There *is* no Wilkinson case. The guy died of natural causes. No evidence of foul play. He was pinned under that wardrobe, nobody came to help him, and he died."

"We know that," Virginia said.

"She means about the house," I said. "About who inherits it—*that* case."

"Sorry, that's not a case either—at least not as far as we're concerned. Did you guys come in through the front door?"

We nodded. Of course, that being the only door, he knew perfectly well we had.

"And the sign outside, did you see it?"

We nodded again.

"And it says, 'Police,' doesn't it?"

Our heads kept bobbing.

"Well," he continued more slowly, "police—like us—investigate crimes and put bad guys in jail. Follow?"

Up, down, up, down.

"There's no crime here." He sat back. I was glad he'd stopped using that patronizing tone of voice. I heard enough of it from Virginia. "It's up to the court to validate that will so Mr. Talbott can have his house."

"Mr. Talbott?" I said. "The house belongs to Jacob Wilkinson."

"Listen, Sergeant Ferreira," Virginia interrupted. "Until just recently, this man we know—his name is Jim . . . uh, James Mandell—was one of New York City's finest. A very smart investigator."

"I hear those New York City cops are pretty crooked," Ferreira said.

I'd heard my dad say the same thing about New Bedford cops, but I decided this wasn't the time to point that out.

"Not this one," Virginia assured him. "You remember the Roscoe Muldoon case a couple of months ago?"

"Sure."

"James Mandell was a leading player in that case—although we were the ones who solved it and exposed Amelia St. Augustine's real killer."

"That so?"

"Yes, and now Mr. Mandell is a . . . a, uh . . ." She looked to me.

"An evidence specialist," was what I blurted out. Stifling the urge to smirk at having rescued Virginia for once, I explained Jimmy's new career to Ferreira.

"That so?" he said again. "He probably charges a lot, and even if this *was* a police matter, I haven't got the budget to go hiring—"

"He'll do it for free," Virginia said quickly.

"What?" I said. "Why would he do that?"

She shot me a searing look that fused my lips. "So you'll call him?" she said to Ferreira. "I know his number. He lives in Fall River."

I knew this would get her nowhere. I bit back an "I told you so," promising myself I'd hold it in at least until we were outside.

"Well," Ferreira said, "if he'll work for free, what have I got to lose? Okay, I'll call him. It'll be worth the trouble just to see the look on the Wilkinson kid's face when he has to admit that Daddy really did leave the house to someone else."

"'The Wilkinson kid'?" I said. "You knew Jacob Wilkinson before this?"

"Oh, yeah. Dragged him in here myself a few times when I was a rookie. He was one wild high school kid. Back during the war, when not too many people had cars, he'd get drunk with his buddies and go racing around town knocking over trash cans, scaring old ladies. And the stealing! Most kids lift a piece of candy now and then. Wilkinson stole boats. He'd go out at night and take other people's boats for joyrides down the river. He even sank one. Old Man Wilkinson paid a bundle for that little adventure. Spoiled rich kid, plain and simple."

It took the rest of the day to round up the necessary people and papers, but Ferreira managed it. As Virginia had predicted, Jimmy welcomed the chance to show off his investigative skills even if he wasn't getting paid. Late in the afternoon, we stood around Ferreira's desk, Jacob and Eddie glaring at each other, Virginia flushed with certainty that she was about to solve the case, and Jimmy clearing his throat repeatedly so we'd all know what a keen professional he was.

"All right, kids, you can go now," Ferreira said.

"But Sergeant—," Virginia began.

"I think we can take it from here." Ferreira looked at us and gave his head a little jerk toward the door.

"Well," she said, and I could almost hear the wheels in her head grinding at full speed. "You'll need some observers, won't you? Someone objective, you know, to keep an eye on, um, this important proceeding here."

"Aw, let the kids stay," Jimmy said, tossing us a sideways look. "They *are* quite observant, I'll guarantee you that." He glanced from Eddie to Jacob, and both nodded.

"Okay," Ferreira said. "You kids can stay. But don't interrupt. Let's just get on with this."

Jimmy laid a typewritten sheet of paper on the desk. "First, we gotta look at the typewriter's characteristics," he said. "Sergeant Ferreira took me over to John Wilkinson's house today, and we typed this with the Royal on the desk in the parlor. You see how the little *e* is kinda shaded in? And how the capital *M* jumps above the line? And look—the *d*, *h*, and *w* are kinda faint compared to the rest. Them's what we call the characteristics."

Virginia looked fascinated. I glanced from Jimmy's paper to Eddie's will and didn't like the direction this was taking.

"And when you look at John Wilkinson's will?" she said. I wished she wouldn't call it that, as if it were the real thing.

"Ahem." Ferreira gave her a threatening look.

"Oh," she said. "Sorry."

"Then we can see them same characteristics," Jimmy went on. We all leaned over and looked. "And the paper itself, you see how it's kinda yellow and a little cracked where it's been folded? The date here at the bottom says nineteen eighteen. In my expert opinion, this will was typed fourteen years ago on the Royal typewriter in John Wilkinson's house." He stood up straight, his bulk giving authority to his words.

"That doesn't prove anything," Jacob Wilkinson said. "It's a fake, I tell you. Look at the signature. That's not my father's handwriting." He pushed his dad's letter toward the will so Jimmy could examine them side by side.

I had a sinking feeling in my stomach as I looked at the two pieces of paper. The handwriting looked the same to me—or close enough to have come from the same hand. The signature on the will was more flamboyant than the writing in the letter, but I could understand that: I embellished my own handwriting whenever I gave people autographs. And Jacob's letter didn't have a real signature to compare, because it was signed simply "Dad."

"Nah," Jimmy said. "You're right. These weren't written by the same person."

"They weren't?" I said.

"How can you tell?" Virginia asked.

"Little differences," Jimmy said. "See the *l* in Wilkinson? Steady pressure on the pen, all the way up and back down. Now look at the *l*s in the letter— they kind of fade at the tail. And the way he joins the *i* and the *n* here"—he pointed to the signature— "has a little twitch, which you see where the *o* and the *n* are joined too. It's not like that in the hand-writing in the letter."

He was right. I could see it too. Now the big

question. "So," I said with a gulp, "which one is real?"

"That I can't say," Jimmy said. "Not without a genuine, guaranteed authentic sample to compare it against. Something that we know for sure was written by John Wilkinson's own hand." He looked at Virginia. She hesitated only a beat.

"His diary," she said. Jimmy nodded, but the rest of us turned and stared at her. Then the questions all burst out at once.

Ferreira: "What diary?"

Jacob: "My father kept a diary?"

Me: "You know where it is?"

Only Eddie was silent.

"Well yes, I guess I do know where it is." Virginia turned a fiery red, and I suddenly understood why she had been smiling that first day when I refused to go back into the house with her. She had known perfectly well I wouldn't go back in there and she would be free to sneak the diary out. "Um, if someone can give me a ride, I can get it right now."

Jimmy volunteered. The rest of us waited in uncomfortable silence while they were gone. Jacob sat down with his letter and read it intently, as if he'd never seen it before. The strange thing was, Eddie did the same with his will. However these two guys felt about each other, I thought, they both cared an awful lot about John Wilkinson, each clinging to a piece of paper as if it were his last link to the man.

The phone's ring startled us out of our reverie. Ferreira grabbed the receiver.

"Weld Street, Ferreira. . . . Yeah. . . . Yeah. . . . All right, I'll tell them." He hung up and looked from Eddie to Jacob. "Well folks, it looks like we haven't solved much of anything. Our young detective went scampering after that crucial piece of evidence, which she expected to find right where she'd hidden it. Only when she got there, it was gone."

# CHAPTER SEVEN

Eddie cast Jacob a defiant look, then turned and hurried out. Ferreira watched him, stone-faced.

"Well," he said, "that sure cleared everything up, didn't it?"

"Thank you for your time, Sergeant Ferreira," Jacob said. "I'll get this straightened out, one way or another. And thank you for . . . taking care of my father's remains. I'll let you know the burial arrangements."

Ferreira hesitated, then said gruffly, "Sure, J. J. You have my condolences."

They shook hands. I was willing to bet they were both remembering the times years ago when a rookie cop had thrown a drunken rich kid into the slammer.

Jimmy and Virginia were just pulling up when Jacob and I walked out of the police station. Jimmy nodded a greeting at us, muttered something about Ferreira, and went inside.

"So where is it?" Virginia said.

"Where's what?" I said.

"You know what. The diary. What did you do with it?"

"What did *I* do with it? You were the one who took it. I thought we agreed to leave it in Mr. Wilkinson's house."

"Whoa, kids," Jacob said. "Wait a minute. Back up. You took my father's diary out of his house?"

Color crept into his face, and Virginia seemed to cower under his werewolf-stare. She actually gulped, apparently realizing for the first time that there was something wrong with what she had done. "We just wanted to find the . . ." The words seemed to strangle in her throat.

"The treasure," I finished for her. "He wrote in the diary that he had a treasure of some kind, and"—I hesitated—"and we had this crazy idea that the two of us could find it." I could feel the wave of gratitude coming off Virginia, although I didn't look at her.

"So you stole his diary and then lost it?" Jacob's voice was rising. "You thought my father had a hidden treasure that *you* could just take?"

I was sure he was going to grab us both by the collar, haul us back into the station, and insist that Ferreira throw us in jail. I wouldn't have blamed him if he did.

"Mr. Wilkinson." Virginia had regained some of her composure. "We never meant to steal anything. We just wanted to find the treasure—and return it to whoever it belonged to."

"And where do you think this treasure might be?" He was still glaring at her, clearly sensing who had really been behind our little caper.

"Well, um, your father wrote a poem explaining what and where it was." She turned to me. "Billy, recite the poem for him."

I did, minus the dramatics. Despite the calm act Virginia was trying to put on for Jacob, I figured her brain had turned to oatmeal and she probably couldn't remember a word of it. By the time I'd finished, he had lost that dangerous look, and I began to breathe a little easier.

"The *Sunset's Glow*," he repeated. "That was his boat."

We waited for more. He was quiet for several seconds before he went on.

"I used to love that boat. It was all teak and cherry wood inside. That's where he got the name from— the colors of that wood."

"He took you out in the boat a lot?" Virginia asked.

His brows bunched together as he gave her a dark look, like he was deciding whether to yell at her again. Then he relaxed. "Whenever he could. It was a business, that boat. Dad had a partner, Captain Randall, who did all the work, taking people out for charter tours or deep-sea fishing. So it wasn't there for us to use all that often. Most of the time, in fact, we only got it in bad weather, when people had canceled their fishing trips."

"Eddie told us he used to work on the boat for your dad," I said.

"Work?" A mirthless half-grin curled his mouth. "Talbott had to work at just staying on his feet. He used to ask my father to let him take the wheel. He almost bashed us on the rocks a few times. He usually got seasick. Dad and I would be fishing over one side while Talbott was throwing up over the other."

"Well," I said, "you'll have the *Sunset's Glow* back, once you get everything straightened out about your dad's will."

Virginia shot me a scorching glare but had enough sense to keep her mouth shut.

"It's funny," Jacob said, gazing into the distance. "You think that death is an ending. But it looks like I have a lot of work ahead of me to clear up my father's estate—after I arrange him a proper burial, of course. He would want to be next to my mother, in Pine Grove Cemetery. Then I'll have to look around his house—maybe there's a *real* will somewhere in there."

I could tell Virginia was biting back a comment.

"Where did he keep the boat?" I said hastily, to protect her from her own big mouth.

"He rented a dock near the Coggeshall Street Bridge. I drove past it this morning."

"And the boat's just sitting there?" I said.

"No, it's not. I don't know what became of it."

The next morning, Dad and I went out back after breakfast and adjusted the boards in our stage to make as smooth a surface as we could. Mom came out a few minutes later, her hands full of things that needed putting away, as always. Virginia was inside, searching for the diary.

"Hey Dad, watch this." I did a few tap steps I'd learned from one of the other kid actors in New York. They came out more like *clump* steps, since I was wearing my Converse sneakers. But I did manage a split at the end—something I'd been practicing every chance I got. I stood and took a bow, and Dad clapped for me.

Mom shook her head. She would like it if Dad and I would forget all about performing and concentrate on getting normal jobs. Dad used to be in vaudeville in Europe and never lost his love for it, but there wasn't much opportunity for a song-and-dance man in New Bedford. He'd supported us by repairing looms at the Grinnell Mill, until he'd lost that job.

"Are the ghosts in your show going to dance like that?" Mom asked.

"Nah. The living people dance. See, that's how they communicate with the ghosts."

Dad laughed and ruffled my hair, then went into the house. Muttering something about Auntie Annie, Mom followed him. I had no sooner started practicing my steps again than when Virginia walked out. I could tell by the look on her face that rehearsal was over. I groaned.

"Did you find it?" I asked.

"Not yet," she said. "Come on. We need to go downtown."

"For what?"

"To look for some record of what happened to Eddie's boat."

I slapped my forehead as melodramatically as I could. "What is the matter with you? It's *not* Eddie's boat, any more than it's Eddie's house or Eddie's treasure. And furthermore, it is *not* any of our business, anyway. I think you should just find the diary, hand it over to Jacob, and butt out."

Half an hour later, we were on a streetcar heading downtown. How do I let her talk me into these things?

We had to ask around at the Customs House

and then the wharf before we finally learned that all the arrivals and departures of boats in New Bedford were recorded in a column in the newspaper called "Marine Journal." We sat ourselves on the hard chairs in the Free Public Library, 1929 newspapers in front of us, and started reading.

After two hours, my shoulders ached and I was so hungry, I could barely see straight. I think that was why my eyes drifted down the page, to where sales were recorded.

"Here it is," I said, reveling in my luck at finding the information that would end this wild-goose chase. "The *Sunset's Glow* arrived on May thirteenth. And then look at this: It was sold the same day, to a Louis Quincy on Oxford Street in Fairhaven. So I guess it's not Eddie's boat or Jacob's, either." I sat back and rubbed my neck, ready to close the big bound newspapers and go home for dinner.

"Sold? Let me see." Virginia ran her finger over the tiny type as she read. "It says it was sold by an Ernest Randall." She looked puzzled.

"The captain," I reminded her. "You know, Mr. Wilkinson's partner."

"Shouldn't Mr. Wilkinson's name be on this?"

I shrugged. "Randall was the one who did all the work. He probably handled all the money, too."

She considered this, then nodded. "No, wait," she said. "The diary. The last entry is dated June second. And in that entry, Mr. Wilkinson wrote about having the boat and planning to sail away on it. Why would he do that?" She got that scary look of excitement in her eyes again. "Unless—"

"Unless he didn't know the boat had been sold?" I said. I had a sinking feeling this discovery was going to lead my partner the sleuth into some new quest and, more to the point, that she was going to drag me along with her.

"Poor Mr. Wilkinson," she said. "No wonder he sounded so angry and sad in his diary. He couldn't count on anyone. His son abandons him, his treacherous partner sells his boat—and probably takes the money and runs. If only Eddie had known how much Mr. Wilkinson needed him."

"Yeah?" I said. "Then where *was* the wonderful Eddie? Why *didn't* he know? And Jacob didn't abandon his father. He tried to keep in touch. He sent pictures of his kids."

"Have you seen these pictures?" she shot back.

"I don't think that ever happened. Jacob walked out on his father and cut him out of his life, and now that there's a house and a treasure to inherit, he's back and acting like Mr. Nice Guy."

This argument was going nowhere, and I was starving. I stifled the urge to reply and instead closed the bound newspapers and stood to leave. She heaved a dramatic sigh, but followed me down the marble stairs and out of the library.

As we walked up William Street toward Sixth, I saw Eddie Talbott hurrying down the steps from the Registry of Deeds, shoving something into his back pocket.

"Eddie," Virginia called, waving to him. She trotted across Sixth to meet him and, of course, I followed. "Hi, Eddie. Guess what we just found out?"

"Hi, kids." He gave her a smile and ruffled my hair. Far too many people do that to me. "Sorry, no time for guessing games. Gotta go."

"Wait, Eddie," she said. "We found something interesting. Where are you going in such a hurry?"

"Okay, I may as well tell you." He threw back his shoulders. "It's all official now—well, almost. The court approved the will, and I've just done the paperwork to have the city register the deed to the house in my name." He paused, then went on more solemnly, "John Wilkinson knew who really cared about him, and it wasn't his son the Harvard snob. *I* was the one who stayed with him. *I* listened to his advice and kept out of trouble. *I* made Mr. Wilkinson proud. He wanted me to have his house. That's why he wrote that will."

"But Eddie—," Virginia began.

"Listen, I do have to get going. I have a lot of cleaning up to do. It really stinks in that house, doesn't it?"

With a wave, he was gone.

# CHAPTER EIGHT

When we got home, my dad asked us to come with him to the Workingman's Club to get some food. My family has never actually gone hungry, but it is always a challenge keeping food on the table. Between the money Virginia's dad sent, the three dollars a week in unemployment we were getting from the city, and the rent from Auntie Annie's other houses, we usually had meat in our Sunday dinners, which was more than a lot of families could say.

Sometimes, though—like this particular Thursday—we ran out of food and money at the same time. My dad's beer wasn't quite ready to sell, and Auntie Annie's tenants were late with their rent again. So off we went to the Workingman's

Club to get some pea soup, bread, and rice pudding. The trip, of course, sent my dad into another one of his tirades about the Depression.

"This can't go on," he said as we drove to the club. "The people won't let it. I think this Roosevelt's got the right idea. Get him into the White House and kick them other buggers out! Hoover's just handing money over to the big bankers while the regular people live in shantytowns. He's inviting them Communists to take over, he is."

I liked being with my dad because I'd been away from home for so long, but these lectures about President Hoover bored me to death. Not so with Virginia, though. She was as big a newspaper fan as my dad.

"I saw a story yesterday about Nazis in New York," she said. "Aunt Trudi actually had some of their leaflets. Those people scare me."

"The Nazis?" Dad pronounced it "nazzies." "We'd better look out if they get control in Germany. They'll soon have us in another war, you'll see."

He and Virginia kept talking politics, but I quit listening. I hoped this little food-gathering mission and the enthralling conversation it started would distract her enough that she wouldn't think about making her daily trip to the former Wilkinson house.

I don't know why it hit me so hard, but I felt crushed that Jacob Wilkinson had not inherited his dad's house after all. Even more upsetting was the realization that if the will was real, Jacob must have been lying, must have faked that letter from his father. How, I wondered, could a father and son let things between them go so sour?

I stewed about it while we collected our rations and all the way home, working up enough of a pout to last the rest of the day.

I should have known Virginia wouldn't let me wallow in my own private drama. She batted the auburn lashes over her gorgeous eyes and declared that we should help poor, unfortunate Eddie clean up that gloomy house. An hour after dinner, I found myself back on my bike pulling up in front of the gate.

Virginia led me onto the piazza and knocked on the door. "Eddie?" she called.

We heard him trotting down the stairs.

"Hiya, kids," he said, pulling the door open a little. "What brings you over here?" He didn't sound very glad to see us.

"We thought you might need some help," Virginia said, eyelashes fluttering.

"Help?"

"Cleaning up," Virginia said.

"Oh. Sure." Eddie looked out past us, toward the sidewalk. "Why don't you bring those bikes around and put them in back of the house. I'd hate to see them stolen."

When we'd done that, he let us in and pushed the front door closed. The scattered papers had been picked up from in front of the door, but other than that, the parlor didn't look much cleaner. Once we were inside, Eddie seemed to warm to us. "Since you're here, come on upstairs and see what I found."

Wishing I'd stayed home to practice my dance steps, I followed him and Virginia up to Mr. Wilkinson's bedroom. The place still gave me the creeps. I didn't think any of us belonged there. I was about to turn around and leave when Eddie said, "There it is—the famous treasure."

For a moment, Virginia and I just stood in the doorway. She was the first to move, stepping slowly around an empty box on the floor and toward the bed, where Eddie had laid out what looked like a bunch of junk. There was some kind of roller with little round indentations all over it, a hand crank, some drawings of a guy in a parachute, a slab of shiny marble, a big thermometer, a couple of spatulas, and a scattering of certificates, folders, and other papers. Eddie looked so proud, I almost felt sorry for him.

"Um, Eddie," Virginia said. "What, um—what is this stuff?"

"It's the stuff fortunes are made of, pretty girl."

Virginia blushed.

"This all belonged to my father," Eddie went on. "He was just about to start a business making cough drops. This was his equipment for cooking and rolling out the candy. And look here—this is his patent on the recipe. Very *secret* recipe. My father came up with it himself. I helped him test it. And here's his trade-marked logo, for Talbott's Mint Drops. Get it? Mint Drops, and it's a guy dropping in a parachute?" Eddie was practically beaming.

It all sounded pretty nutty to me. I couldn't imagine that *this* was the treasure Mr. Wilkinson had planned to sail away with. It might be a good idea and all, but a bunch of equipment and a good idea was still a long way from anything you could use to pay your rent.

I could see the doubt on Virginia's face, too, even though she obviously wanted to believe in Eddie. "Gee, Eddie," she said. "Gosh. Candy, huh? Gee."

It was the second time in two days I'd seen her at a loss for words. I cherished the moment, knowing it wouldn't last.

"My father had plans, big plans. He worked for years to buy this equipment and get all the right documents. Everything was ready to go."

"Well then, why did Mr. Wilkinson have all this stuff?" I said.

Eddie suddenly looked deflated. "Oh, my dad had some financial trouble he hadn't expected. He needed money quick. So he borrowed it from Mr. Wilkinson and left all this for collateral. He died before he could repay Mr. Wilkinson. But Mr. Wilkinson was a smart man. He knew the value of what my father had worked for. He said so in that poem.

'Riches sweet, swelled with time.
My stock in trade, treasure is mine.

No one knows, no one sees,
Rolling and cool, gold it shall be.'

See? He's talking about cool mint candy, about rolling it out onto this marble slab. That's how it's done. And he knows it's going to bring him riches." Eddie scowled. "He was going to take my father's work and turn it into a fortune for himself." Then he raised his eyebrows and said, "But then again, he didn't know where to find me. I'm sure Mr. Wilkinson never meant to cut me out of the treasure my father left."

"Where was all this?" Virginia asked.

"Ah," Eddie said. "The end of the poem explains that.

'The answer to a sailor's pain
Awaits beyond the *Sunset's Glow.*'"

He walked over to the painting opposite the foot of the bed, grabbed one side of it, and swung it out from the wall. Behind it was a cabinet door with its lock broken out. "He kept it all in here. All except the marble slab. That was on the floor where his body was found. I'm guessing it was up on the shelf in the wardrobe. Must have been what made it top-heavy enough to fall."

Eddie began taking the stuff from the bed and laying it in the box on the floor. He handled each piece like priceless jewelry. Virginia looked at me, shrugged, and moved to help him.

"No!" he said, blocking her. "I mean, thanks, but I can handle this myself. Listen, I really have a lot to do here. You kids better get on home. I appreciate your help in all this—finding Mr. Wilkinson, and bringing in that New York guy to show J. J. up for the phony he is. I've spent a lot of time riding in freight cars and walking from house to house looking for work or a meal while J. J. lived the high life in Boston. If it weren't for you two, I'd just have more of that to look forward to."

He guided us out of the bedroom and down the stairs.

"Looks like your case is closed, Miss Detective." He cast Virginia a smile. "See you around."

"So," I said as we headed around the house to fetch our bikes. "Case closed. Some treasure that was."

"Well, Eddie obviously considers it a treasure," she said. "I wonder if Jacob would have felt the same way about that stuff?"

"I bet Jacob would have remembered the poem right," I said.

"What do you mean?"

"Aw, Eddie messed up a line, that's all."

"Which line?"

"'Nobody knows, nobody sees.' It's supposed to be 'No one's to know, no one's to sea.' It's the one where Mr. Wilkinson spelled 'see' wrong, remember?"

"Oh, yeah," she said. She grabbed her bike's handlebars and pulled it away from the wall, then stopped. "Billy, recite the whole thing again, will you?"

> "'Riches sweet, swelled with time.
> My stock in trade, treasure is mine.
> No one's to know, no one's to sea,
> Rolling and cool, gold it shall be.
> At grieving's end, a world to gain,
> The greatest treasure man can know.
> The answer to a sailor's pain
> Awaits beyond the *Sunset's Glow.*'"

"'The greatest treasure man can know'?" she said. "That candy-making stuff? I don't believe it."

"That's the most sensible thing you've said in a week," I said, trying not be smug. I scooted my bike away from the house and turned it to leave the yard.

"The treasure is something else."

I stopped. "Oh, no. Case closed, Sherlock. Eddie got his house and a treasure he's satisfied with, and we know all we need to know. Let's go home and get to work on our show."

"Billy, think about it. Swells, rolling and cool, a sailor—what do those things have in common?"

"Would it do me any good to say 'nothing'?"

"The sea," she continued. "The s-e-a kind of sea."

"So?"

"So that stuff upstairs isn't the treasure Mr. Wilkinson was writing about. There's another treasure—a *real* treasure."

I could see where this was heading. I debated whether to try to resist, which in the end would be pointless, or to just go along now. "All right," I said. "There's a real treasure somewhere else. So we're back where we were the day we found Mr. Wilkinson. We don't know what it is or where it is." I knew I would regret my next question. "Now what?"

"The sea," she repeated. "That's the answer. 'Beyond the *Sunset's Glow*.' If we can find that boat, I'm sure we'll find the real treasure."

# CHAPTER NINE

As we rode our bikes down Acushnet Avenue, I told Virginia a little about Fairhaven, the town where the new owner of the *Sunset's Glow* supposedly lived.

"First," I instructed her, "you don't pronounce it FAIR-hay-ven. It's feh-HAY-ven.

"The section where this Quincy guy lives—if he's still living there—is the oldest part of town. It goes back way before the Revolutionary War. People call it Poverty Point because they used to build ships there until the shipbuilders went out of business."

"Because of the Depression, you mean?"

"Nah, they had to close after the bridge was built downriver. Once the bridge went up, they couldn't get big ships in and out anymore. That was more than a hundred years ago."

We turned left on Coggeshall Street, rode across the Acushnet River and into Fairhaven, then headed south toward Poverty Point.

The newspaper item we'd found in the library hadn't given a full address for Louis Quincy, so we parked our bikes and started looking for someone we could ask about him. We found a couple of kids running around playing a tag game. One of them got hold of the other's arm and yelled, "One, two, three! Caught by me!" They were playing a game I liked to play with my neighborhood pals, called "release." The guy who was "it" had to catch the other guys and put them in a certain spot, but the ones who were still free could sneak up and free the ones who'd been caught. I didn't know how they managed the game with only two people, but seeing these kids play "Release" made me wish this whole goofy treasure hunt were over so I could go play with my pals.

"Hey, kids," Virginia called, like she was much older than they were. They quit playing as we walked up. "Do you boys live around here?"

Both kids were blond-haired and freckle-faced. The bigger one looked about our age, the other one a few years younger. They glanced at each other, and then the smaller one said, "Yeah. Why?"

"We're looking for a man who owns a pretty boat," she said. "His name is Louis Quincy. Do you know where he lives?"

"Right over there," the little kid said, pointing, before the bigger one shot an elbow into his shoulder. "Ow!"

"Why do you want to know?" the bigger kid said, his eyes narrowing.

"Our dad owes him some money," I said. "He sent us to arrange the payment, but he couldn't remember Mr. Quincy's exact address." I looked toward where the smaller kid had pointed. "In that house? The red one with the white trim?"

The big kid looked at the little one, then back at me. He nodded.

"Thanks," I said.

I could feel their gaze following us as we turned and walked toward the Quincy house. When we got closer, I could see that it had been recently painted. Parked next to it was a big, shiny Pierce-Arrow, almost the same dark red as the house. I thought it was an odd car to have in this neighborhood—first, because the streets were barely wide enough to contain it, and second, who in Poverty Point could afford a car like that?

We knocked on the door and waited. After a few seconds, a woman opened the door. She was about my mom's age, but taller and more slender. Her brown hair curved across half of her forehead and around her face, and she wore a dress like the ones the stores were advertising for the new season.

"Yes?" she said, not exactly hostile but not what you'd call welcoming, either.

"Mrs. Quincy?" Virginia asked, in her best movie-star polite voice.

"Yes."

"My name is Virginia, and this is my brother Billy." Mrs. Quincy and I smiled and nodded at each other. "And we're looking for a boat that your husband bought about three years ago. The *Sunset's Glow*. Our father is interested in buying the boat, and he sent us over to take a look at it first. He's so busy at work, you see, that he couldn't come himself. But he heard the *Sunset's Glow* is such a lovely fishing boat and, well, we wanted a nice boat for our family to use this summer."

EILEEN HEYES

It was a pretty limp story. I figured she was making it up on the spot.

"Well . . ." Mrs. Quincy turned away and we heard her say, "Did you tell someone you wanted to sell your boat?"

A deeper voice grumbled a response that didn't sound much like "Certainly dear, tell the nice kids to go have a look."

We heard heavy footsteps, then a man appeared at the door and the woman stepped aside. He was a little shorter than she was, and stocky. His clothes were clean, but from his smell I imagined he hadn't bathed quite as recently as his wife had. "What do you want with my boat?" he said.

"Well, as I was telling Mrs. Quincy, our father—"

"How old are you kids, anyway?"

"Eleven," I said, wondering what this had to do with anything.

"It's not for sale. At any price." He stepped back, and the heavy white door slammed in our faces.

We looked at each other for a stunned moment, then turned and headed back to where we had left the bikes.

"What do you think he's hiding?" Virginia said finally.

I shrugged. "Maybe he just doesn't want to sell his boat."

There were six kids standing around the bikes, including the two we had talked to before. Three of the others were maybe nine or ten, and the other one looked about seven years old.

"These yours?" asked the little one who'd pointed out the house.

"Yeah," I said.

"Want to try them?" Virginia said.

I looked at her in surprise, but she shot me a quick, silencing glance. Then I caught on to what she was planning.

"Yeah," I said. "Go ahead. Everyone gets a turn." I grinned, something I had learned to do convincingly no matter what. I could see the relief on Virginia's face when she realized I was with her.

The little blond kid and his older brother were the first to try the bikes, but one by one the rest of the boys took a ride up and down the street, laughing and making imitation engine noises. We let them get good and tired. After what seemed like hours, they all quit and gathered around us and the bikes again, smiling and chatting like we were their new best friends.

"Do you all live here on Oxford Street?" If anyone could turn the conversation where we wanted it to go, I knew Virginia could.

"Most of us," said the first big kid, whose name was Joey. "Ronnie and Gus live over on Cherry."

"It's an interesting neighborhood," she went on. "I've never been over here before. Until Dad sent us today."

"You say your dad owes Mr. Quincy some money?" Joey asked. Hearing this, the kids exchanged knowing looks.

"Why, yes," Virginia said.

"He let us have some fish on credit," I added helpfully.

They burst out laughing.

"Oh," the one named Andy said with a smirk. "Was it Bass?"

"Or White Label?" Gus said.

At this, they all laughed again. Virginia looked at me in bewilderment. I'd caught on, and I figured she would pretty quickly.

Finally, Ronnie said to her, "You don't know? Bass—it's a kind of ale. And White Label?" He slapped his forehead. "Booze!"

"Look," Joey said, "never mind. Forget we said anything."

"Oh, I knew that," Virginia said, as if it had only been the brand names that had confused her. "Our dad said Mr. Quincy must be a pretty good, uh, boat driver, to stay clear of the Coast Guard in a boat like the *Sunset's Glow.*"

"It's called the *Starbuck* now," Gus said.

"Like the first mate in *Moby Dick*?" I said.

Gus shrugged. "And Mr. Quincy's had it fixed up a little since he got it."

"Guys," Joey said, his voice a warning.

"Yeah," Andy said, ignoring him. "Three Liberty aircraft engines, four hundred horsepower each—"

"Got 'em from government surplus," Ronnie put in. "Can you believe that?"

"He doesn't just stay clear of the Coast Guard, he outruns 'em like they were on tugboats. Vrrrrrm!" Gus stuck out his hand, palm down, and shot it across in front of himself, by way of demonstration.

"Wow," I said, "sounds like it's even more swell

than our dad said. Where's it docked?"

"Up the bank from the Edgewater house." Andy tipped his head toward the end of the street, where a big old house sat beside the river. We could see across to the New Bedford side, where a row of idle cotton mill buildings stood, a silent reminder that there were plenty more poor people outside of Poverty Point.

"You want to play release with us?" asked Joey's little brother, Skip.

I was about to accept, but Virginia said, "Gosh, we can't today. We have to go tell Dad about the arrangements we made, you know, for him to settle up with Mr. Quincy. But thanks, anyway." She gave them a coquettish starlet kind of smile, and the weirdest thing happened: Joey and Ronnie smiled back like they were, I don't know, charmed or something.

The little kids started pulling the others away, back to their game. We waved, then jumped on the bikes and headed for home.

"I wonder if Mr. Wilkinson's treasure is on the boat?" I said as we pushed the bikes into Auntie

Annie's cluttered little garage. We often left them out, but the sky was darkening with thick clouds, and we didn't want our own two-wheeled treasures to get rained on.

"You do?" She looked at me like I'd just told her I wished I could grow a third nostril.

"Yeah. Don't you?"

"Well sure, but I didn't think you were interested in this case."

"And *I* didn't know we were investigating a rumrunner. This is a whole different thing." We sat on the step outside the back door. "Boy, I'd love to get a good look at a rumrunner's boat. Those guys tear out the insides and put in double hulls and secret compartments to hide the liquor in. And armor plating—some of them have armor plating on the pilothouse."

"Billy, how do you know all this?"

"Oh, don't you read the paper?" I said with a little smirk. "That front-page story the other day talked about all the stuff they do. I should have known when I saw that fancy car that Quincy wasn't making a living fishing."

"Wait a minute," she said. "If he's torn out the

**EILEEN HEYES**

insides, then even if the treasure *was* there before, it's probably long gone now. And Quincy's not about to tell us what he did with it."

"You're not saying you're ready to give up?"

"What choice do we have? He's had the boat for three years. He had three aircraft engines put into it. He's probably yanked out all that nice teak and cherry wood. How could any treasure possibly still be hidden on it? I bet he found the treasure and sold it, or spent it, long ago."

I refused to believe she wanted to quit just when I was getting ready to pursue answers. "I've got an idea. Rumrunners go out by the dark of the moon, and the moon's practically full now. So Quincy won't be anywhere near his boat. We can check it out tonight."

The door creaked open, and we leaned aside so my dad could get down the steps. "Check what out?" he said.

Virginia looked to me for a cue.

"A boat over in Fairhaven, Dad. We met some kids at Poverty Point today, and they invited us to come back and see their father's fishing boat." I hated lying to Dad, but I knew we'd never get out if I told

him the truth. And after the whole Maureen inci-
dent, I had promised not to keep anything from him
again. I felt like scum.

"What's this fisherman's name? I know a couple
of fellas over there."

"Quincy," I said. "His kids say the boat looks
grand by moonlight."

"Won't be much moonlight tonight, with all
these clouds. How about we make this our cards
night, since Virginia goes to synagogue tomorrow?"

"Oh, you don't have to do that," Virginia said.
"I—I can skip Friday services this week. We can play
cards tomorrow night. It's just that we told those kids
we'd come back tonight."

Dad looked at us like he wanted to ask more.
But, as usual, he let it drop. "Suit yourselves," he said
with a shrug, and disappeared around the corner of
the house.

"Okay," Virginia said when he'd gone. "Let's do
it. We'll bring flashlights, and some tools."

"Tools?"

"In case we have to open any secret compartments."

Virginia has a cop's instinct for this kind of stuff.

Her hunches had turned out to be pretty close to the truth on our last case.

Close—but just far enough off that they'd almost gotten us killed.

"Virginia," I said. "Reassure me on this."

"What?"

"This isn't going to be dangerous, is it?"

"Dangerous?" At the word, her eyes took on that old gleam of excitement. "Of course not, Billy. Not dangerous at all."

# CHAPTER TEN

The distance from my house to Poverty Point seemed like a million miles in the dark. I carried the hammer, wrench, and screwdriver tied up in a bundle on the back of my bike. We each held a flashlight, but we only used them for the especially dark stretches to preserve the batteries. Virginia had insisted we put some soot from the stove all over our faces so we'd have a better chance of sneaking around undetected. I think she saw that in a movie once.

As my dad had predicted, the moon was mostly hidden behind clouds, peeking out only occasionally as if to check on us. A cool breeze blew in off Buzzards Bay, and we could smell the ocean spray.

This far up the river, though, the water remained pretty placid.

We pedaled toward some trees upriver from the Edgewater house, parked the bikes behind a big clump of bushes, and trudged down to the dock on the riverbank.

"There," Virginia said, pointing her flashlight. "*Starbuck*. That's it."

I guessed the boat to be about forty feet long, its pilothouse cutting a fairly low profile. I felt a thrill pulse through me at the thought of three aircraft engines propelling this fishing boat through the night, defying the waves, daring any Coast Guard captain to catch it.

Holding one of the dock's pilings for balance, we clambered onto the *Starbuck* and began examining the deck for some part that might have been untouched for three years. Near the stern, I found fishing equipment. Had the kids been playing us for fools? Was this Quincy guy really just a very successful fisherman? I looked more closely. The equipment was pristine, as if it had never actually touched a fish—or even salt water, for that matter.

Now I understood. The gear was just for cover. "Nothing very promising back here," I said.

"The poem said it was 'beyond the *Sunset's Glow.*' Maybe he meant all the way behind the boat. Look over the back, see if you see anything that might be a secret compartment."

As if three aircraft engines could have been installed without such a compartment being found. Still, I scrambled to the edge with my light and peered down. Where the word "Starbuck" was painted, I could see the slightly raised remains of the old name. It had not been scraped off, but merely covered over. "I don't see anything," I said, pushing myself up.

Suddenly Virginia was next to me, snatching my flashlight and shutting it off.

"Hey," I protested.

"Shhh. I heard something."

We stood motionless. My senses prickled as I strained to hear over the lapping of the river against the boat. Then I caught it too—a rustle of bushes, then footsteps on the road coming toward us. The steps grew quiet, and I knew whoever it was had reached the grass that lay between the road and the dock.

Virginia pulled me toward the hatch that led below the deck.

"Wait," I whispered. "The tools."

Without turning our lights back on, we felt around frantically. I must have jumped a foot when she grabbed my arm.

"Got 'em," she whispered. "Quick. In here."

We fumbled down into the darkness of the cabin just as we heard the first footstep on the wooden dock.

"It must be Quincy," I whispered.

"What do we do?"

"Stay calm and quiet. He won't make a liquor run by the full moon, even if it's cloudy. He's just checking on his boat. Shhh."

The footsteps came closer. Not heavy, confident steps, but light ones, as if Quincy was afraid someone might hear him on the dock. I peeked through one of the small windows high up in the cabin, careful not to get near enough that he would be able to see me from outside. The boat tipped toward the dock, and I could see his feet climbing aboard.

Seconds later, Quincy grabbed the hatch cover and swung it shut. His catlike footsteps moved about the deck. I was glad we'd remembered to grab the tools. Finally, he stopped not far from the hatch. We heard fumbling and clicking.

Then, with a rumble, the engines started.

"What do we do?" Even in Virginia's quiet whisper, I could hear her panic. My partner the would-be cop had a nasty habit of losing her composure at the first sign of danger.

"Shh," I whispered back. "Feel around those windows. Maybe they have curtains or something and we can cover them up." I knew from experience that this would help calm her down. Virginia Grady, woman of action.

We each took a side of the cabin, reaching up and sliding dark shades across the windows. They fit snugly. *Of course,* I thought. *This boat has to be able to move through the water without any light showing from it.*

Above the engines' hum, we could hear Quincy untie the *Starbuck* and drop the ropes onto the deck. The boat rocked as we felt him pull it away from the dock and out onto the Acushnet River. The craft leaned into a left turn.

"He's heading down the river," I said, though I knew Virginia could figure this out.

"Why is it so quiet?" she asked. "Shouldn't three aircraft engines make enough noise to wake the whole neighborhood?"

"I don't think anyone in this neighborhood would find it strange to hear a boat leaving at this time of night. And it's probably got silencers."

"Silencers? I guess this is also something you read in the paper?"

I ignored the question and clicked on my flashlight. "Let's look for the treasure. This might be our only chance."

Even with my puny bit of boating experience, I could tell this wasn't your average cabin. No kitchen, no place to sleep or eat. In the middle stood something squarish and bulky covered with canvas. We edged around it and unlatched a cabinet on the left side of the boat. Inside were long rolls of paper.

"Maps," she said, and I nodded. I could figure that out too. She stuck her hand in and felt the inside walls of the cabinet. "No other openings."

We made our way around the cabin, opening each storage space, looking or feeling for what might be a secret compartment. Behind the door that led toward the front of the boat was a large, empty area that ended in the **V** shape of the bow. It had a flat floor built into it.

"This is where he stashes the booze," I said. "Take a whiff. You can smell it."

Virginia stuck her head in and inhaled deeply, then pulled out, coughing.

"Shhh!" I said.

She got herself under control. Even in the dim light, I could tell she was giving me one of her dark looks.

On the right side of the cabin, we found something that made us gasp.

"Would ya look at that," I said. My hand trembling, I reached out to stroke the guns that lay menacingly inside this locker. There were two sawed-off shotguns, several handguns, and even a submachine gun. "Quincy doesn't mean to get caught, does he?"

We stared at each other in the dusky light, then instinctively looked up. Quincy—the guy who was somewhere over our heads, piloting this boat with its twelve hundred horsepower out toward the bay. I think we'd both forgotten about him.

As if to remind us, the engines began to hum louder, and the boat picked up speed.

"Stay calm," I said. "He doesn't know we're here. We'll just find what we're after, and then. . . ."

Virginia waited, wide-eyed, for me to finish this reassuring sentence.

I realized that I didn't know *what then*.

And then . . . we would burst out of the cabin, jump over the side, and swim to shore before he even saw us?

And then . . . we would leap out onto the deck, overpower Quincy, tie him up, and pilot ourselves safely back up the river?

Oh yeah, that was plausible. I could see us doing that.

And then . . . more likely, we would cower like bilge rats in the deepest, darkest corner of his booze-smuggling locker and hope we didn't get knocked out by the liquor fumes before he left the boat and we could sneak off.

"And then . . ." I squared my skinny shoulders, trying to act tougher than I felt. "We'll think of something."

She accepted this without comment. We returned to our search, reaching carefully behind and beneath all those guns, then moving farther around the cabin's periphery. Toward the stern, we found another big boozy-smelling locker with a couple of valvelike things in its far corners.

Finally we turned to the bulk in the middle of the cabin and pulled off its canvas covering. Once again, we both sucked in our breath.

It was a table with a short rim around its edges and cabinets underneath. The entire fixture was made of a polished reddish wood. "The sunset's glow—the wood," I said softly. "It's still here."

We looked at each other. She said it first: "Then the treasure might be too."

A jolt of energy shot through me. My heart began to race. For the first time, I really cared about finding this treasure, whatever it was.

We searched each compartment, one by one. The smaller ones held some cleats, batteries, slender ropes, and things we couldn't identify but decided were probably spare parts for those big engines. We also found some small, heavy boxes that got us pretty excited—until we realized that they held not gold doubloons but bullets. The cabinet under the table on my side held a life preserver ring that still had the boat's old name stenciled on it.

The *Starbuck* sped up more.

"The engine's making a funny sound," Virginia said. "Billy, I don't like this."

I listened. The sound came again, a deeper rumbling than the Liberties' hum. "That's not the engines," I said. "That's thunder."

We switched off our lights and pulled ourselves up high enough to push aside a black shade and peek out. The sky flashed white, sliced by lightning, and more thunder rolled across the water. I could see lights on the shore, and I guessed we were nearly through New Bedford Harbor and heading much too swiftly out to Buzzards Bay.

The hatch flew open.

"All right, kids," a voice called. "Game's over. Come on out."

"Eddie!" Virginia yelled. "What are you doing here?"

"Out, I said."

We turned to each other. I could see my alarm reflected in her face, but her eyes also held something like relief. Or hope.

Not knowing what else to do, we climbed out on deck.

"Eddie," Virginia said, "what are you doing on this boat?"

He throttled up and turned too hard into the waves, steering out toward the ocean and nearly dumping us all overboard as he did. "Whoa. This boat never moved like this in the old days." He pointed toward the stern. "Sit." Eddie straightened the *Starbuck* and clutched the wheel with one hand, the pilothouse frame with the other. "The *Sunset's Glow* should have been mine. I just came to claim it."

"But how did you ever find it?" Virginia said, managing to sound almost admiring. I didn't think Eddie would fall for this, but it was worth a try.

"How? You led me right to it. I gotta hand it to you kids. You're pretty good detectives. Except that you need to learn to look out for someone tailing you." He swallowed hard, as another explosion of lightning made it daytime on the deck for an instant. "So, did you find the real treasure?"

"Real treasure?" I said. "What real treasure?"

"Don't try to con me. I heard you two talking after you left Mr. Wilkinson's house today. So I had the poem wrong, huh?" He glared at me. "So you think J. J. would have remembered it the right way?"

He gulped again, his grip tightening on the pilot-house door. I remembered what Jacob had said about their childhood fishing trips.

More lightning, and now big raindrops began to pelt us.

"Answer my question," Eddie said. "Did you find it?"

Then I heard it. Over the rain, the thunder, and the hum of the *Starbuck*'s Liberties. It was another engine, big and loud, somewhere behind us.

I turned, clicked on my flashlight, and waved it at the sound. "Here! We're here!"

Before I could get another word out, I felt the light wrenched from my hand. Eddie flung it into the roiling water behind us, then grabbed me by the shoulders and spun me around to face him.

"That's enough, kid. I oughta throw you over too." He shook me. "Forget about the Coast Guard. If they catch up, none of us will get anything." He let me go and backed off, grabbing the wheel and looking from me to Virginia. His voice was more reasonable as he continued.

"Listen kids, we can work together, okay? We're gonna get this tub out of here, and once we're far enough away, we'll all look for the treasure. When we find it, I'll give you a share, how's that? And then you can go home. And I'll head off into the sunset with my boat and the rest of my treasure. Okay?"

"Sure, Eddie," Virginia said immediately. "Okay. That sounds like a good plan. Doesn't it, Billy?"

"Yeah," I said, trying to sound sincere. "Good plan."

"Let's start looking right away." She whipped her flashlight around and shined the light in Eddie's face.

His hand flew up to cover his eyes.

I bolted to the wheel, shoved him aside, and turned it hard right. Eddie stumbled toward the stern and fell. In a moment Virginia was at my side, rain dripping down her face. She kept the light, the only weapon we had, pointed at Eddie's face. I churned the *Starbuck* from side to side, rocking it as wildly as I could.

Eddie clutched the deck rail and pulled himself to his feet. Even by the flashlight's beam I could see his face had gone gray. It was working.

"Urgh," he moaned. He lurched to the rail and leaned over, his body heaving.

"Turn her around," Virginia shouted. "Head back up the river."

I pulled the wheel to the right, shore lights sliding across the horizon as I pointed the *Starbuck* back toward home.

At that moment, Eddie lunged for the wheel, knocking us both out of his way. The flashlight slipped from Virginia's hand and slid through the open cabin hatch.

"Get down there and stay out of my way!" Eddie shouted. He pushed me toward the hatch, and I jumped through it to keep from falling. Virginia practically landed on top of me. The cover slammed behind us, and we heard a latch click.

We sat stunned for a moment, feeling the *Starbuck* turn back out to sea.

Finally Virginia said, "Nice try. It almost worked."

We could hear the growl of the Coast Guard boat getting louder as it gained on us. In a matter of minutes, I was sure, we would be saved.

Then the *Starbuck*'s engines hummed louder, and we felt her slam through the waves as she picked up speed. A lot of speed.

"Oh, no," I groaned. "This boat's outfitted to carry a full load of booze and still outrun the Coast Guard."

"And Eddie's figured out how fast it can go. We don't stand a chance of getting rescued now, do we?"

"Not a chance," I said. "Unless. . . ." I didn't like the idea that had popped into my head. Did not like it at all.

"Unless what?" Virginia grabbed me by my suspenders.

"Hey, leggo."

She did.

"Unless," I went on, "we can stop it ourselves."

"But how? Eddie's out there at the throttle, and we're trapped down here."

I gulped and told her my idea.

"Are you crazy? We'll drown if we do that!"

The *Starbuck* jolted from side to side, tossing us against the lockers.

"And if we don't try it, he might just throw us overboard, anyway," I said.

She flipped on the flashlight, and our eyes met. We spoke in unison: "Let's do it."

We scrambled toward the back booze locker,

opened it, and crawled inside. I could feel the power-
ful engines vibrating beneath us. "Turn them slowly,"
I said. "That'll give us our best chance of—" I
couldn't finish.

"Of surviving?"

"Yeah," I said weakly.

I'd read about this trick of the rumrunners: They
had valves installed so that, if they had no chance of
escaping the Coast Guard, as a last resort they could
open the valves and sink their boat with all its illegal
cargo. We each grabbed one of the seacocks in the
back of the compartment and strained to turn it.

"I can't move it," she said.

"I can't either. Keep trying!"

We both grunted with the struggle. My hands
ached as I poured all my strength into it. Suddenly,
mine gave. I heard water rushing in below. "Got it,"
I said. "Come on, let's get out of here."

"Wait—just—Billy, come help me."

I scooted over and grabbed the seacock, and we
pushed together.

"There!" she said. "Let's go."

I could feel the *Starbuck* slowing already, her back
end dropping as the engine room took on water.

Virginia grabbed the flashlight, and we scrambled forward. While she retrieved our bundle of tools, I yanked open the cabinet with the life preserver and grabbed it. "Hey, it won't come out," I shouted.

In an instant she was at my side, helping me pull. "We've got to get it out," she said.

I felt around on the floor for our tools. I wedged the screwdriver into the cabinet's back panel, where the life preserver was attached, and pounded it with the hammer. With a couple of knocks, the whole panel came loose, and we fell back holding it.

"Billy, look!" She shined the light into the broken cupboard. In the darkness behind where the panel had been was a wooden chest not much bigger than a bread box.

"'Beyond the *Sunset's Glow.*'" I turned the light onto the life preserver so she could see the words stenciled on it. "This is it. Wilkinson's treasure."

We dropped the light and the life preserver and pulled together, sliding the chest out of its hiding place. It wasn't heavy.

The engines began to sputter. The back of the boat sank farther, and I could tell it had slowed down a lot. I found the strap that held the life preserver to the broken panel and I yanked it off.

"Jeez, we've gotta go. The water's coming into that back booze compartment. Go shoot the hatch open."

"Me? I don't know how to use a gun. I thought you were going to shoot it open."

We looked at each other in horror.

I grabbed the hammer and rushed to the steps, clutching the life preserver. "Arrrrgh," I yelled, banging on the hatch cover with all my might. I could hear Eddie overhead, cursing and stumbling. Finally, the hatch cover flew open. "Come on," I yelled to Virginia. "Let's go."

When I emerged onto the deck, she was at my heels, the treasure chest in her arms.

"What did you do to my boat?" Eddie shouted. "It's sinking."

At that moment, the engines gave a final spit and went silent. Rain pouring on our heads again, we backed away from Eddie, toward the bow, as the boat continued its descent. I could hear the rumble of another engine in the distance. Eddie started toward us. "Is that it?" he said to Virginia. "Is that the real treasure?" He leaped forward and tried to grab it.

Virginia dodged sideways, stumbling against the

rail. "Billy!" she yelled. Then she disappeared over the side, taking the chest with her.

"Virginia," I called. Eddie stood between me and the rail Virginia had fallen over. I made a quick choice. "I'll save you," I yelled, and jumped into the dark water.

No sooner had I spotted her than I heard another splash behind me. The life preserver under one arm, I swam frantically toward Virginia. Then something pushed my head down under the water. I felt the ring jerked from my grip. When I came up, coughing for air, Eddie had the life preserver and was heading for Virginia.

I yelled his name, and he turned. With no better ideas, I splashed the salty water at his eyes. In two strokes he was back in front of me. He pushed me under again. I flailed and clawed, trying to knock his hand off my head. My chest ached as I struggled to hang on to the air I'd gulped into my lungs. Things got wacky in my head. The water seemed to rumble and grow light, and I thought I heard something else splash in right near us.

The Grim Reaper, I knew, had come to get me. I quit struggling. Everything went black.

EILEEN HEYES

# CHAPTER ELEVEN

I woke up in a room with a single lightbulb hanging overhead. As my vision cleared, I could see flyspecks on the white walls. Then, above me, the worried face of my dad came into focus.

"He's coming to," Dad said to someone. A couple of men in uniforms appeared, Virginia right behind them. "Billy, can you hear me?"

"I hear you, Dad." I tried to sit myself up.

Dad pulled me toward him and hugged me so hard, I thought I might suffocate. I didn't care. I hugged him back just as hard, feeling tears spring to my eyes. From the shaking of his body, I knew he was crying too.

Dad let go and looked at my face, pushing damp

hair from my forehead. He turned toward Virginia and reached out, and she came over to share a hug too. She sat at my feet. Her hair was damp like mine, her face still sooty around the edges.

"Where am I?" I said.

"You're in the Coast Guard station, son," one of the uniformed guys said. "I'm Captain Halloran. You gave us quite a scare. We were afraid we'd lost you."

"I wasn't going to let that happen," Dad said. "No one's going to hurt you anymore, not whilst I've got anything to say about it."

He and Virginia both wore ill-fitting but dry clothes. I seemed to have a big shirt on, but nothing else. I pulled the cot's scratchy blanket more securely around my waist.

"We were just about to board the *Starbuck* when you went over the side. Then your dad saw that Talbott guy snatch the life preserver and push you under. Before we could stop him, he'd jumped in the water after you."

Dad pulled me to him again.

"But Virginia," I said. "How did you—?"

"The chest," she said. "Remember how light it was? It floated. I just had to hang on."

"We fished her out pretty quick," Captain Halloran said. "And got all of you onto our cutter before the rumrunner went under."

"What were you doing with the Coast Guard, Dad?" I asked.

"I got worried about you two going out so late, and that story about the boat was a bit goofy. So I called the Coast Guard, and they knew the boat and Quincy. They also knew it was no fishing boat."

"Your dad talked us into cruising up to check things out and insisted on coming with us. Then we saw the *Starbuck* tearing across the harbor toward the bay."

"Eddie—?"

"Downtown," Halloran said. "In jail. I had to feel kinda sorry for the guy. He wasn't like the others we haul in. The real bad guys are defiant and the fishermen are pretty good-natured, like the chase is just a game. This Talbott guy, though, seemed like he was really ashamed. Kept saying he never meant to hurt anyone, all he wanted was his treasure. You kids know what he was talking about, I presume?"

Virginia and I looked at each other, a quick silent

agreement cementing between us. I let her do the talking.

"It was some candy-making equipment that used to belong to his father," she said. "It had been in John Wilkinson's house, and Eddie Talbott wanted it back. He wanted to start up the candy business his father had dreamed of. It meant a lot to him."

"Well," Halloran said, "if he had it on that boat with him, it's gone now."

One of the other Coast Guard guys scared up some pants for me, and then they gave us all a ride back to Auntie Annie's house. No one said a word when Virginia grabbed the wooden chest and carried it out like it had been hers all along.

The next morning after breakfast, we settled down on the piazza with another screwdriver—having lost my dad's favorite one on the *Starbuck*—and went to work on the treasure chest.

"This is sealed all the way around," I said, trying to pry it open.

"That's why it didn't fill with water," Virginia said. "Kind of like . . ."

"Like what?" I said when it became clear she didn't plan on finishing the thought.

"Maybe we shouldn't do this."

"Like what?" I stopped jimmying the screwdriver.

"Like the cannibal's coffin in *Moby Dick*. Remember how the book ends? The main character survives by clinging to the coffin."

I rolled my eyes. "This isn't a coffin. It's a treasure chest. And we're gonna see what's inside of it."

Just then Jacob Wilkinson pulled up at the curb, followed by Sergeant Ferreira and Jimmy Mandell in a police car. At the same time, Dad came around the corner of the house. And Mom appeared from the front door. It was like someone had announced a party and all the guests arrived at once.

Virginia made the introductions. My mom offered our visitors some tea, but they all declined.

"I got a call this morning from a Captain Halloran of the Coast Guard," Jacob said. "He told me about what happened to the *Sunset's Glow*."

I took a deep breath, then filled him in on what we'd found at the library and what we had learned from the kids at Poverty Point.

"Twelve hundred horsepower?" He sounded incredulous. "On *that* boat? No wonder the Coast Guard couldn't catch it—until you two came along, that is."

"And we found this," I said. "We think it might be your dad's treasure."

He sat on the steps and examined the chest, then took the screwdriver and, with a few quick motions, pried the chest open. We all leaned over to see the riches John Wilkinson had planned to sail away with.

"Stock certificates," Jacob said, pulling out papers.

Virginia and I exchanged a look. "His 'stock in trade,'" I recalled. "Like the poem said."

"Ten thousand shares of The Chelsea Bank and Trust," Jacob went on. "Ten thousand of Amalgamated Textile, twenty thousand of Fordyce and Templeton Stores, twenty thousand of Bank of the United States. This is amazing." He looked at each of us. "This is a side of my father I never saw."

"You didn't know he owned stocks?" Virginia said.

"Bank of the United States?" my dad said. "That went under a couple years ago."

Jacob nodded. "Every one of these companies has

gone bankrupt since the crash of twenty-nine. These certificates are worthless. That's what I mean. My dad was so shrewd with his money. I never saw him make a bad investment in my life."

"He never knew they were bad," Virginia said. "He died before the crash. He wrote in his diary about having 'The greatest treasure man can know.'"

I saw something else in the chest. I pulled out an envelope and handed it to Jacob. "It's addressed to you."

He tore it open and scanned the letter inside. When he spoke, his voice was husky. "He was going to come to Boston on the *Sunset's Glow* and see me and Carmen. He was ready to forgive everything, if I would forgive him, so we could be a real family. Here's what he says at the end: 'I had planned to mail this to you, but I've decided I must deliver these words in person. I must see your face and'"—his voice broke—"'and put my arms around you. For you are my son, my life, and always will be.'" Jacob wiped a tear that was about to escape down his cheek.

"That's what he meant," Dad said, coming up onto the piazza. He stroked my hair. "You were his treasure, Jacob."

"But what about the will?" I said. "Why did Mr. Wilkinson leave everything to Eddie?"

"Ahem," Ferreira broke in. "The will was fake after all. I questioned Talbott a little while ago. He admitted everything."

"But we saw Eddie downtown yesterday," Virginia said. "He said the court approved the will and the city was going to—"

Ferreira waved dismissively. "Some young courthouse clerk thought it was a routine thing. The Registry of Deeds wouldn't have let him take the house, though. They're pretty careful with property deeds."

"That's why he was so nervous," I said. "He made us put our bikes in back when we went to visit yesterday so it would look like no one was at the house."

"He wanted to get his father's stuff out before anyone could catch him there," Virginia said. "He knew he wasn't going to end up with the house at all."

"But the will," I said. "Jimmy, you said it was typed on Mr. Wilkinson's typewriter fourteen years ago."

"It was," Jimmy said.

"Apparently," Ferreira said, "once J. J. went away to Harvard, Talbott did some very wishful thinking."

"That sounds like Eddie," Jacob said, nodding. "He was always trying to worm into our life. His own father could never seem to make anything work out right, so Eddie always wished he was in my family instead. I thought it was fun when we were kids. But it annoyed me more and more, the older we got. The thing was, my dad encouraged this whole fantasy of Eddie's. Even when I stayed out with my high school pals, Dad would have Eddie over at the house."

"So Eddie typed the will himself, just pretending Mr. Wilkinson was going to leave everything to him?" Virginia said.

"That's right," Ferreira said. "He had taught himself to do a pretty good imitation of Wilkinson's signature. And he kept that piece of paper all those years. The past few months, since he's been back in New Bedford, he's been hanging around the Wilkinson house, looking in the windows. But he didn't dare go inside until you kids found Mr. Wilkinson and the remains were taken away."

I remembered how the bushy yard had been trampled. It had been Eddie snooping around. And almost every time we went to the Wilkinson house, Eddie was there. "Why did he leave town in the first place?"

"Shame," Ferreira said. "He ran up some debts playing dice. His father had to borrow a thousand dollars from Wilkinson to keep the thugs from breaking Eddie's legs. He died in nineteen twenty-four, still owing Wilkinson the money. But Eddie couldn't face Wilkinson, so he left town and didn't come back until a few months ago. He's been staying in the blockses—"

"Blockses?" Virginia said.

"Places the mills built for the workers to live in," I told her. "These plain brick buildings that look like big blocks."

"And we found all his candy-making equipment there."

"Bill," Auntie Annie hollered from inside the house, "you've a phone call."

Dad went to answer it.

"We also found this." Ferreira handed Jacob another letter.

Jacob turned it over a few times, then opened it. "My letter. With the pictures of my son."

"He must have picked up whatever old mail was on the floor when he was there yesterday," Ferreira said.

"So the only mystery left," Virginia said, "is—"

"Whatever happened to the diary?" I finished.

Mom cleared her throat. "I have it."

"What?" Virginia and I turned to her.

"Well, you see, I was tidying up a bit." She lowered her voice. "You know how our Annie gets when things are lying about."

We nodded.

"It was under the couch where Virginia sleeps. So I just put it on the bookshelf and forgot it. After Virginia and Jimmy come in fussing about a book the other day, I remembered. Here it is." She handed the brown book to Jacob. "I'm so sorry about your father."

"Thank you, Mrs. O'Dwyer." He handled it like it was gold. "And I thank you kids, too. You're pretty good treasure hunters. I guess your summer will be pretty boring after all this excitement, huh?"

"Nope." Dad burst through the door. "No time to be bored." He grinned, drawing out his dramatic moment. Dad's a showman, through and through.

"That was Roscoe Muldoon. Him and his buddies are starting up the 'Rusty and Fred' pictures again. And he wants you two in New York a week from Monday."

Virginia and I looked at each other. We both leaped to our feet at once and snared Mom and Dad into a big hug.

"Hey," I said, pulling away, "we'd better hurry if we're gonna get our show on before then."

"We never did find enough props," Virginia said, right with me, just like always.

"A serious problem," I said, nodding gravely. "Cobwebs would be nice. Some old, dusty books, maybe. But I think what we really need . . ."

They all watched me.

"What we really need is a skeleton."

DEAR READER:

This book was something of a family history project for me. If you've read the first O'Dwyer & Grady mystery, *Acting Innocent*, you know that the character of Billy is based on my father, William Heyes. My research for this book sent me to my father's hometown. Some of New Bedford looked much as it had when he was growing up in the 1930s: the public library, Abraham Lincoln School, and Dad's old neighborhood. The places my father lived in—the tenement on Query Street and the Glennon Street house of his own aunt Annie—still stand.

Early in the twentieth century, the people of New Bedford were hugely dependent on the town's cotton mills for work. In the 1920s the cotton industry went through changes that put many mills out of business and many people out of work. This, in turn, hurt other businesses, including fishing. Thus, some fishermen in the New Bedford area who could no longer make a living by selling fish put their boats to use smuggling liquor.

I have many people to thank for helping me with this book. The New Bedford Free Public Library's awesome research librarian, Paul Cyr, led me to answers about everything from rumrunners to the synagogue Virginia would attend. (It, too, still stands, though it is now a Pentacostal church.) Bob and Georgette Mogilnicki gave generously of their time and energy, showing me around and filling in details of daily life. At the New Bedford Visitors Center, Lucy Bly and Ed Baldwin offered insights, as did Elaine Forgue of Abraham Lincoln School. I've taken some small liberties with things like dates and geography, for which I hope the good people of New Bedford and Fairhaven will forgive me.

I am also grateful to the writer friends who helped me turn vague ideas into a story, and then turn a rough manuscript into a smooth one: Candy Dahl, Donna Sink, the Triangle Circle, and the Sisters Four.

Any errors that remain are my own.

*Eileen Heyes*

# Test your detective skills with these spine-tingling Aladdin Mysteries!

he Star-Spangled Secret
By K. M. Kimball

Mystery at Kittiwake Bay
By Joyce Stengel

Scared Stiff
By Willo Davis Roberts

O'Dwyer & Grady
Starring in Acting Innocent
By Eileen Heyes

Ghosts in the Gallery
By Barbara Brooks Wallace

## The York Trilogy By Phyllis Reynolds Naylor

Shadows on the Wall

Faces in the Water

Footprints at the Window